Hood Snitch

Author;
Josip Ćaran

Zagreb
2022

It's extremely hard to catch a good spy.
You wouldn't believe in an excellent one, even if they
told you about him.

<u>Josip Ćaran</u>

Impressum

Title; Hood snitch

Author; Josip Ćaran

Proofreading & Editing; Art prijevodi d.o.o.

Illustrations; www.dizajnerica.hr

Type of publication; A spy thriller

Place and year of publication; Zagreb, 2022

Number of pages; 177

Publisher; Author's personal publications

ISBN; 978-953-50187-2-8

I

"Volkswagen caught in a lie – the value of shares fell by twenty percent... Moody's downgraded Russia's credit rating... In six years of recession, more than 200,000 jobs have been lost." – TV news drives me crazy. Why doesn't Mum at least turn the volume down, if she has to watch that crap? I'm a mess already, so they don't have to go to the trouble of putting it in my ears so that it rings in my head. As if I don't know that the recession has taken its toll in the whole country, as well as in the whole Europe. Due to the financial crisis in the USA, the global financial crisis is shaking us all. I've been out of work for four years now. As of March 2011, the unemployment rate has risen to a staggering twenty percent. I no longer believe that I could find a decent job. I'm up to my throat in shit anyway...

- Dominik, come! Let's eat! It will cool down.

- I'm not in the mood now, Mum.

- Come on, son, I've made your favourite pie. It won't be tasty when it cools down. Come on... I've prepared it the way you like it.

I have to get out of this. My heart breaks for my old Mum.

- Fuck, Mum, can you turn the TV down a bit? - Damn it, I really hate it when I yell at her like that, but why can't she keep quiet. And that damn TV...

- What's wrong, son? Why are you yelling at your Mum?

- I'm sorry, Ma, come here - I lower my voice, poor woman, it's not her fault: - Come, sit – she sits next to my pillow and puts her head in my lap. She strokes my hair, just like when I was a kid.

- Why are you nervous, son?

- I didn't get enough sleep, Ma. Come on, please, turn that TV off.

- Ok, son. Let's eat. Do you want me to bring the pie here?

"Filip Krovinović signs for Hajduk..."

- Turn it up, Ma! - I yell at her because football news is what I'm really interested in. I am an ardent fan of the football club Dinamo Zagreb. I guess I was attracted by the fact that my father was a soccer legend in the eighties. There's so much left of him in me and it seems like that's the only thing worth a damn.

- Dominik, for God's sake, a minute ago you sent me to turn the tone down.

- I want to hear this, Ma. You can turn off the TV afterwards.

- Do you want to eat here or...?

- Shut up... - I don't believe it, I yelled again: - I'm sorry, Ma, come here. - I can read the news later on my mobile phone.

- This pie is really good – I am talking with my mouth full to comfort her, while I chew a piece that I tore from my greasy hand with my teeth, like an animal.

I keep staring into void and absentmindedly stuff that pie into my mouth, while in my head I compose myself and shuffle my life through a thousand twists and turns, and the only road I want to follow is the one that will bring me freedom. I am twenty-five years old, and what have I done with my life? Nothing, zero. I live on social aid, my father's pocket money and the neighbourhood combinations.

- Son, why are you unhappy?

I live with my mother in the house because the old man remarried...

- Son?

- Aa... What were you saying, Mum?! Sorry, I was in my own thoughts. What did you say?

- Why are you unhappy?

- I'm not unhappy, Ma. I'm thinking about what to do. I can no longer depend on social aid like this and wait for my old man to give me pocket money, as if I am incapable.

- There will be work, son. Do not worry. Uncle called; he shall pay us a visit today.
- Nice, mother, but I have to go look for work.

My uncle is a good man. He's helped me a lot. I worked for him for a long time until the recession took its toll. I worked in the commercial department. It was a reputable construction company, and that's where I draw a positive image of myself among the world. But it, too, has long since failed, as has my uncle – he can't earn enough nor can he compose himself, and he begins to give away mentally. Everything in this country has gone downhill. But at least they experienced something, but where are we going? It's no wonder that young people indulge in narcotics or burn themselves out.

- Well, son, you could stay at least a little while to see your uncle. He hasn't been here for a long time.
- Next time, Ma. I really have to go now.

I still do not move my eyes fixed on one point. And I don't notice that my other cell phone is ringing. I have two cell phones; one is for communication with the Cop, an old Nokia 3310, so that no one could track our conversations. Even so, I have to be vigilant and keep communication on the phone to a minimum, because you never know if someone is eavesdropping or maybe someone has discovered a way to track that old device as well. For a long time, those Nokias have been used for secret communication between criminals. I'm lucky that I communicate with the Cop, so he's careful and covers all tracks.

- Son? Son? - The old Ma starts waving her hand in front of my eyes because I don't feel her at all.
- Huh?
- Your cell phone is ringing.
- Yes, a cell phone.

Damn it. The Cop is calling me.

- I have to go, Ma.

I reject the call and send a text message that I will call back in a few minutes, when I am alone. First, I go behind the building and light a cigarette. I need a little more time to gather myself before I call him.

I've been working as a hood snitch for the Cop since he caught me four years ago. The Cop caught me with an illegal gun, and it was either prison or I had to work for him. I had no choice. My Mum would burst if they put me behind bars. She lost enough of her nerves with my old man anyway. She should have left him earlier, and she's still annoyed by everything. A womanizer – he hung around brothels more than with her. Now he has a new family and is living his own life. If he wasn't giving me money, I would forget him too.

The cell phone is ringing again. I have to answer now. The Cop might think I'm doing something wrong, and then I'm dead.

- Yes?
- At noon. You know the place. Be prompt. - hang up.

II

With the termination of the telephone connection, I exhale the air accumulated in my lungs. It seemed to me that my heart wanted to jump out. I'm always afraid that this obese complex guy will expose me for having kept something from him. He is such a greedy man and I am not surprised at all that his wife left him. I'm convinced she was heavily drugged before she could even marry him. The fat bearded man raised his nose to the heavens, parting the clouds, flaunting his title of middle inspector like a peacock, as if he were the president with his head and beard, and if he had any sense, he wouldn't hide his head with that huge beard. He's got the world by its balls to catch me in his net, so now he's exploiting me for pittance, but my five minutes will come. I will take my revenge on that slob. I will no longer spend my days snitching on everything and everyone. I can't bear to commit petty theft, rob kiosks, and I don't want to be found out about planning football riots and drug dealing either. I can no longer risk my life and the life of my mother. She didn't deserve it, and neither did I. Do innocent people always have to suffer the consequences of recession caused by political figures?!

I glance at the digital clock on my cell phone. There are still seven minutes until noon. I light a cigarette to stay with my thoughts a little longer and look at the sky, as I stare at the ceiling every night while lying in bed and I remember all those poor people I imprisoned with my snitching, people who believed me and told me everything because no one could have imagined that I would work for the cops. I can't take this anymore, and I can't count on anyone but myself. The blue of the sky stretches far beyond my sight and smells of freedom that seems just as far away. I dream of moving away, but I realize that it's not very realistic because I'm aware that the Cop would snitch on me and then I fucked up. The old man would kill me first, and I would also be a target for all those I cheated on, and they would pursue me for the rest of my life. There has to be a way to get out of this though.

I meet the Cop every Tuesday in the garage complex that separates the buildings in my neighbourhood. Communication on the phone is kept to a minimum so that no one would stalk us, and he is also afraid that I might snitch on him somewhere. Recently, he calls me less often. I feel that I'm not that important to him anymore and that he's running out of material where he could show himself to be someone and something. A common slob. He is barely making ends meet. No one in town can figure him out because he struts around like a peacock with that badge and doesn't let the people breathe. Sold soul! Cop asshole!

I throw a cigarette butt on the concrete and stomp on it, turning my strong foot left and right while imagining that I'm squeezing the Cop's head, no prettier than a pig's. I would prefer to step on it and never watch it again. It's a minute to noon. I drag myself lazily towards the garage. There has to be some way to get out of this.

III

Peter Horvat, middle inspector at the police station in east Zagreb. He always wanted to become a cop. He was one of those kids who never got a chance to be a thief in the cops and thieves' game and had a heck of a time being chased by others. It always belonged to him to be a stalker and snitch, the kids didn't like him because he was a fat, selfish complainer. He had to accept these roles in order to be involved in the games at all. Later, he got used to it and vowed to himself that when he grows up, he will be a police officer and put behind bars all those who teased him when he was a kid, to get revenge on them.

- Peter Shit-eater, Peter Shit-eater... - he was haunted by the provoking voices of his peers through his memory. Even after more than thirty-five years, he could not erase that burden of non-acceptance. All he ever wanted was to be part of a group, to be loved and admired, but he was never able to achieve that.

In the house, he was treated like an ugly duckling. His father died when he was only nine months old, his mother soon remarried and gave birth to a son and a daughter who were always more of a priority than him. The stepfather didn't care about him yet. When his mother was not at home, he used to call him a fat pig and make him crouch in the corner for the slightest wrong look or movement, while his bro and sister played and turned the house upside down. Out of anger and helplessness, he continued to eat even more and thus gained weight and gave others a reason to call him all kinds of derogatory names. Back then, as a very small boy, he vowed to enforce justice and become someone and something. Unfortunately, this desire for justice and acceptance became his illness and obsession.

- Give me the ball, Momo.
- Get to me first, Fat...
- Do we want to play three-on-three basketball?
- I can be with you too.
- Well, you see there's no room?! And you, fat man, how do you intend to run?... The only thing is that you serve us as a mattress, so that we can bounce and dunk on more easily... hahaha

Their voices growled through his mind like hyenas, and it seemed to him that they had claws, long sharp claws that dug deep under his skin and stayed there, like parasites. There was no way he could get rid of them.

When he entered puberty, he started running and took care of his diet, with the intention of entering law enforcement. He promised himself: - I will expel you freaks! You will see who Peter Horvat is. I will repay you a hundredfold for all that you have done to me.

He barely passed the entrance exam. Last on the list. Fortunately for him at that time, it wasn't a particularly popular occupation, his mother at that time was flirting with a sleazy inspector who seemed to be some guy in Zagreb, so he also pushed it a little to get him accepted. His colleagues started teasing him during the exam. During the physical fitness test, you could hear whispers from the guys pushing each other in line:

- Look at this nerd.
- I bet he can't run at all.
- Come on, push the pig...
- Silence there, we start with checking the basic motor status. As you know, the first exercise: endurance test of arm and shoulder girdle strength...
- I bet a fat man can't do a single push up…

- I said silence! One more word and you'll be disqualified.

Peter did all the exercises with difficulty, but he was stubborn and persistent, and Weasel, as his mother's lover was called in the end, stood behind him.

IV

The garage is huge, in a semi-rut condition, and also serves as a nuclear shelter. I always enter through the back door. First, I look around me several times and make sure that no one is following me, and when I am sure that no one is, I slowly slip in through the back door. The Cop is already waiting for me behind the boxes. He always parks a little further away and we are by the stairs: he on the outside, and I on the inside, by the stairs in the hallway and the entrance. It's ideal because we can talk and exchange money, and it's dark enough that no one can see my face. I don't know who is doing all this nonsense!

- Has anyone seen you? - is the first thing he asked me in a whisper.
- No one did - I say.

- Safe? - He looked at me questioningly, while, like a lie detector, he scanned my face.

- Safe. - I say again.

- Um... good. - Pretend to be strict, but I see that I have convinced him that everything is clean: - And what do you have for me? - He asks again.

- Fans are planning riots for Saturday's Dinamo-Rijeka derby.

- It was already hinted at.

- Where? What time?

- It will start in the stands, towards the end of the first part of the match. - I'm broadcasting everything, and if I could, I'd be the first to go and start a riot at that match, but I can't. I sniped the info from the BBB fan leader as a joke. We drank a couple of beers on the bench in front of the building and he told me everything himself when he saw how crazy I was about football and Dinamo. I never even ask for information on a topic because that's how I give myself away. I just let people tell me for themselves. So, I'm not suspicious anywhere. On top of that, I've been at this for so long that I've become a real expert on human psychology and behaviour.

- Is there anything else? - he scans me again with that dog look.
- No. - I'm lying.
- Are you sure? You haven't heard anything about those boxes of cigarettes that disappeared from the warehouse of Petey's shop?
- I did not, I swear. - I replied. Some kid from the neighbourhood stole them. Dealing around. Poor guy, he lives alone with his immobile mother, his old man passed away a long time ago. They don't even have bread. I feel so sorry for that family. The recession is the worst economic crisis in the last hundred years. People have lost face and honour, just like me.
- Good. See that you find out something about it by next Tuesday. Beat it, I don't want to look at you.

I get out of the garage and blow out the air again, as if I had been inflated before, like a balloon. I feel so relieved when I manage to keep the Cop quiet, I feel very sorry for some people.

I light another cigarette. There must be a way out of this situation.

V

- Look at that little pig! - Peter remembered the calls of his peers while he was stacking files in his office: - Now I like you, Momo.
- Shut up, I heard that Weasel is standing behind him.
- Come on! What do I care?! What can Slime do to me?! Now look at this: - Pigs, pigs, deadline, deadline... Peter Shit-eater, Peter the Pig... - his peers shouted after him while in uniform, after just completed training, he was walking through town with his first (and almost only) girlfriend. Later, he had another one, whom he quickly married, but she also left him and ran away with her lover, less than a month after the wedding.

He turned to threaten them with his finger: - You will see... The girl immediately understood what it was about. She spent that afternoon with him and never heard from him again.

Since then, his life's mission has been to put as many rascals as possible behind bars and devote himself completely to the advancement of the service.

- I need this guy, Dominik Braun. He's scared of me; I can do with him as I want. - He thought.

Peter lived alone. A small studio apartment: a bed, a TV and a mini kitchen with a microwave in which he heated up the food he bought. He rarely saw his mother, once every two months. After Weasel, she soon found another suitor, so he also scorned him because of her for a while, but luckily, he quickly retired. Over time, Peter began to identify with him, it was his defence mechanism. He would no longer be a victim, but a bully, he believed that a change of role would bring him happiness, and thus a mass of petty criminals perished, while the big ones managed to get away with it again.

VI

I became a rogue. I can't look at myself in the mirror. I go to the store on the ground floor of the building and buy two beers. It has become a sneaky habit of mine; someone always sneaks up and sits next to me drinking in the yard and confesses his "sins" to me with a spit.

The kid I spared from the cops a while ago is walking by.

- Where have you been, kid? What's up?

- Hi, Dominik, bro. - he answered me a little thoughtfully, and I felt sorry for him: - Let's have a beer. - I invite him, although I probably can't extract any new information from him that I would like to tell the Cop. It's over my head. I guess I can drink one beer with my head relieved, as much as possible.

He sits next to me, as if he was just waiting for that. I act as a trustworthy person, someone who knows how to listen and does not object. If, God forbid, it was otherwise, I would have gone to the other world a long time ago, or I would have been shot by the Cop or by those I cheated on.

- You want a cigarette, bro? - He asks me, and I accept.

We sit like that in silence and smoke, each lost in his own thoughts.

- How's your Mum? - I ask purely for the sake of conversation, to break the silence.
- Good. - He can barely say it, and I can see that it's not quite like that and that it's bothering him a lot.
- Did you find a job?

- No. - He says and looks at a point on the ground:
  - I don't have money for medicine for the old Ma,
  Dominik. I don't know what to do. I sold all the
  tobacco, but that's not enough for us even for the
  basics of life. Have you started working?

Poor guy, I think, at least I have a living, unlike him, and my old Ma can still take care of herself. I only have my own worries to worry about, but as I got myself into this, I have to get out. I feel that now is the right moment, when I am no longer so important to the Cop.

- I didn't find anything either, I told him: - Don't
  worry, something will come up, I console him.

Then a white Renault Master van is parked in front of the building. Plates are Bosnian, but some Arabs come out of it, at least that's how they look to me. There are four of them, about forty years old and one younger and stunted. They open the back door and take out some packages that they carry towards the garage.

- Who are these, I wonder out loud and look pale at
  the kid.
- Aaa... they moved in a few days ago, he answers
  disinterestedly.
- So, what are they doing there? - I'm surprised.
- I have no idea. - he says disinterestedly.

Out of the store comes Tony, a rogue from the area, an old man who does nothing, knows everything and pokes his nose everywhere. He is carrying a bag with juice and chips in his hand.

- What's up, guys? - he addresses us.
- Nothing, Tony. Here we sit and drink beer.
- And can old Tony sit down with you? I have chips. Goes well with beer.

I couldn't stand the old leaf. That one had a nose to stick where the worst bigmouth wouldn't, but I often sat with him because I would always get a signal from him where to look for material to snitch on a cop. And now I was really wondering who these Arabs were, and I believed that he certainly knew something.

- Sit down, Tony. We're out of beer, sorry.
- Don't worry, kid. I bought myself some juice, he says and begins the story, looking after the Arabs, without even sitting down: - These came from Bosnia. Dangerously capable, he says: - The recession hit us all in the pocket and forced us to tighten our belts, and they are opening a game room with billiards and slot machines.

The kid's eyes glaze over at the mention of the playhouse because he sees an opportunity to collect some money for the old Ma's medicine in a short time, but he remains silent, he doesn't ask anything. I don't think it's a smart idea for him, but due to the financial crisis, I've buried myself in much bigger shit, so I don't even look at him crosswise, and I'm interested in hearing more about the newcomers, so I wouldn't want to interrupt old Tony.

- Good merchants, no problem, the old man continues the story: - They have companies all over the Balkans and the Adriatic, and they sell every grocery item. There's nothing they can't get you, and everything is fair and clean. And our poor Croatian people, hey...

Just like that, hey, I think.

- Where did you learn all this, Tony? - asks the kid, visibly interested.
- Ah, Uncle Tony knows everything, kid. Old age wisdom, the old man flaunts. And nothing is happening with you, huh?
- Nothing, Tony, same as every day. - I say, and the little one is also silent because he is not in the mood to tell Tony about his problems, since the whole neighbourhood would know about it right away.

- Ah, well... I'm leaving now, he immediately picked himself up when he saw that there was nothing he could sniff.

The kid and I stay there for a while and smoke in silence, and then we each go our separate ways, preoccupied with our own ordeal.

VII

They did not like Peter even in the Cop station where he worked. His sick superior value complex got on everyone's nerves, so they avoided him and plotted against him, which encouraged him even more to prove himself and chase ranks in order to create an image of himself as someone of worth.

- What is this, Peter? - The senior inspector would often yell at him.

He would then curl up like a cricket, tuck his head between his shoulders like a turtle and apologize from below: - Well... well, that... Well, that's...

- I'm asking you nicely, what is this? Answer me! What are you doing?

- Oh, excuse me, Inspector. Looks like I was wrong. Will not be repeated.
- And you'd better not let it happen again, otherwise... next time ten percent of the crying, and if, God forbid, this continues... the act goes away... whoosh... like one or two...
- Oh, please don't. - He would bend down and put his palms together to pray to him.
- Dude, get out of my office. To work! I don't want to see you here, you puss! Do what you're paid to do. Otherwise, you know what awaits you. Got it?
- Yes, I got it. - he retreated like a worm towards the door.

Colleagues watched all this through the barely ajar door of the office or from the corners of the corridor where they would find themselves as if by chance when Peter went out. They watched and laughed mischievously because they didn't really like him.

He noticed what they were doing, so he would use the first opportunity when the senior inspector was not there to bully and harass his lower rank.

- Kid, come here! This is how it's gonna be, huh? - Not infrequently, he used to slap someone in the face with a sneer or beat him around with a baton.

Some would later complain to a senior inspector. Peter denied that it was true, so later he would bother them again for snitching on him, and so it would go round and round forever.

VIII

A few weeks later.

- Dominik, get up! It's noon. - the old Ma calls me. I'm in my bed on my back. I covered my face with my forearm because I can't even look at the little sun that breaks through the rickety, dilapidated wooden blinds.
- Dominik! - she keeps calling me.
I lazily remove my hand from my face and continue to lie and stare at the ceiling, as usual.
- Son, it's noon. Would you like breakfast?
I hate to answer her so much. I have no desire for anything anymore. I would prefer to disappear, just to find peace. I reach my hand above my head and feel for my cell phone. Jesus Christ, it's Tuesday! Noon! The Cop will bury me. I jump out of bed like a fury and put on the first thing I find in the closet.

- I have to go, Ma. - I kiss her on the forehead and head towards the door.
- Wait, son, you haven't eaten! Where are you going? At least drink coffee.
- I have a job interview, Mum. I completely forgot. I will later.
- So, wait, where are you going in shorts? Son! - she keeps shouting after me, but I'm already at the exit of the building and running towards the garage.

The Cop is already inside with a junior assistant. Thank God, it doesn't look like he missed me too much. I see that they are very busy with something, so I guess he didn't even notice that I was a little late. I stood there hidden like that for five minutes until the Cop sent the kid to the car. His junior assistant leaves, extremely disinterested, sits in the car and stares at the phone, you can see that he is fed up with everything and that the Cop officer is disgusted by him. I entered the garage quietly, without saying a word. I stood there again for a while until Peter noticed me.

- Oh, Dominik, you've arrived. Sorry, I got a little carried away with the little one.

Why is he so nice today? He must have had a good catch.

- And what are you bringing me? - he asked.
- Tonight, at nine at the old oak, handover of ecstasy candies.
- Oh, fine, fine. - he rubs his palms. And he doesn't ask if there's anything else, I can see that he's on cloud nine when he hears this information. and that he's in a hurry.
- Come on, I have to go, Anthony (junior partner) is waiting for me..

I'll stay in the garage a little longer. I feel miserable, as I do after every snitch. I hope the Cop didn't reveal my identity to little Anthony. The story could easily be expanded at the end, and that does not work in my favour, not now that I am a few steps away from freedom. What I learned from my grandfather, my mother's father, and made a vow to myself as a kid, so much so that it became my character trait, is that I will never allow life to play with me and call it a dare, but that I will harness my muscles and fight on my own to stand in the way of every misfortune and so-called bad luck. That must be the case this time as well. I will crush the recession head and tail, I will be victorious, I will be free. I sit on the stairs and light a cigarette. I stare into space as I try to lift myself to feel less miserable. Just as I got up to go home, I heard some rustling.

- I, sick, packed, there are eight boxes - I hear them talking and I understand from the accent that the man is from Bosnia.
- Come on, Fatih, pack up. We're finishing up. - a man with an Arabic accent tells him.
- I'm going, sick.

I believe that these are the Arabs that little Damir and I saw in the parking lot in front of the building a few weeks ago. They store goods here. I'm staying a little longer to smoke and answer some text messages.

A few moments later I smelled a strange smell. I strain my nose a little, smell it again and feel that it is marijuana. Someone is smoking there, but I don't know who. I turned in the direction where the smell was coming from and finally saw a Bosnian man of my age sitting on the boxes and smoking.

That's it, I thought to myself: It's a card that will help me get closer to the Arabs, through this Bosnian guy and pot. I don't know why I want to meet them, but I feel that they can help me get out of this.

I exited the garage through another door to walk past him and try to make any kind of contact.

- Hi, bro. - I said to him in passing: Are you enjoying yourself?
- Me, a little bit, it was time. - he didn't invite me to join him, but I saw that he was looking at me favourably, but he was already quite busy, so he probably didn't even think that I could keep him company, and he probably also wanted to inquire about me in more details, if possible, to check if I'm not some scumbag or a thief.

IX

Peter was satisfied and went to the senior inspector to report what he found out. He was still smiling from the door. He entered with his head held high, strutting like a peacock.

- Good afternoon, inspector.
- Peter, wait outside, I have to have an important conversation with Denis.

This one had already mowed him down like a cold shower. Denis Vuković was his colleague, with whom he was forever competing in the service, and this one always escaped him by a hair's breadth, which annoyed Peter very much. By the way, Denis was a favourite of the senior inspector, while he really took Peter to heart. So, Denis, with very little effort, more with his charm than with his work, quickly reached the desired position and was a favourite among his colleagues - he really knew how to get under people's skin, while Peter worked day and night, but was always frowning, cold and asocial, constantly was an apostate and hated in society.

After waiting for almost half an hour, the senior inspector finally invited him inside. This one immediately began with the story of how he had done a great deed, as if he had discovered a crime of world proportions.

- You see, inspectors, that gang, they hide so skilfully, no one has been able to discover them so far, but I...
- Peter, don't choke and don't choke! - the senior inspector was angry: - Let me hear who and what it is about.
- Well, now... - he was already confused: - Well, near the old oak trees by the lake in Maksimir, tonight at 9:00 pm...
- Handover of ecstasy candy?

- How do you know?

- Denis told me now. You have to be a little more up-to-date. Come, run, so that my eyes no longer see you here today!

Peter bowed and went outside. How can someone ruin his catch and pleasure like that?! He hated Denis, the senior inspector, all of them. It would be his favourite if they didn't exist, he only needed them to have someone to envy him, to prove to himself that he is someone and something.

X

I go back to the apartment. The old Ma went for a walk. There is hot coffee, fried cheese and a couple of boiled eggs on the table. She always thinks about me, I'm just ashamed in front of her. She thinks I spend my days looking for a job, and I embarrass her and myself for pittance.

I put a few bites in my mouth and went on Facebook on my mobile to look for the Bosnian. It seems to me that the Arab called him "Fatih". I type that name into the search engine.

- Let's see... - I say in a low voice: - aha... here, Fatih Hodžić, Fatih Bašić... it's not that one... Abdullah - well, it could be this one. - I click on the profile photo to determine if it is Fatih I am looking for. - This picture is a bit blurry, but I think it's him. I'll wait until I see the other pictures... Aha... Here he is - I shout out loud, and then put my fist over my mouth, aware that the terrace door is open and the whole neighbourhood could hear me.

I'm sending Fatih a friend request. I continue my breakfast, but I'm impatient and every now and then I check to see if he accepted me as a friend. I walk around the apartment, check Facebook again, lie down in bed, stare at the ceiling, check Facebook again, then get up and look for something sweet in the fridge, then go back to bed and check Facebook, get up to drink water, check Facebook... and so on until the evening. Somewhere around seven o'clock in the evening, I finally see that Fatih has accepted me. I'm lit up like Christmas lights, I finally see a bright spot at the end of this dark tunnel of my life.

I immediately sent him a message via Messenger: - Hello, Fatih. Thank you for the friendship. I live next door.

We can drink beer together and watch the game if you're up for it.

I am pleasantly surprised by the almost simultaneous answer: - Thank you too, Dominik. You can always count on me, but only in the evening since I'm on my job with my old man during the day. Write to me here.

I liked his message. If nothing works out, at least I'll have another buddy to watch the game and drink beer with. And those Arabs seem like completely OK characters to me, something in me tells me that they will be my ticket to the world of freedom. I scroll through Fatih's Facebook profile to see what he likes. Ten days have passed. It's Sunday. I haven't invited him to bleat together yet. We met several times in the garage, exchanged greetings and that was it. I have to come up with something good to gain his trust and thus get closer to the Arabs. The first impression is the most important. When he feels that there is a friend in me, he will give me all the information I need. And they will never suspect me. In the end, the long-term experience of a police informant speaks to me - How did I not remember this earlier? - I wonder! The most effective way to get close to someone is to selflessly help them. Just so the Cop doesn't find out. He would ruin everything for me. I won't write anything to

Fatih, I'm waiting to meet him again in the garage. The first contact is recorded in the brain as crucial for creating an image of the other, that's why I decide to make it face to face, where I will present myself in the best light.

XI

Peter was sitting in his office somewhat electrified because Denis had won the laurels again. He flipped through the files and plucked strands of balding short brown hair as if he was brushing his ears, and then he would cross his fists, then snap his fingers and let out some strange cries stretching his lower lip: - ppppp... If someone was watching that scene from the side, you might think that a nervous patient, although that was not so far from the truth.

- He will tell me... that little bastard... a snot nose... he thinks someone is stupid... uh... - he got angry, then slammed his fist on the table.

At that moment, there was a knock at the door. It was his colleague, Denis.

- Peter, may I come in?
- What do you want, barking bastard? - he hissed to himself, he didn't dare to speak out loud so that

someone wouldn't hear him, so that he would jeopardize his position. Then he faked a smile and politely answered: - Yes, of course, Denis, here you go.

- The inspector is sending me. You know about the case from last night.
- Yes, Peter nodded.
- The inspector told me that you are also familiar with it. - continued Denis: - I would like us to work together on that case. He said that if we clean up everyone associated with that gang, we'll both be candidates for the position of Senior Inspector.
- Oh sure, Denis. - said Peter, visibly delighted by the opportunity that was being presented to him, but greed was speaking in him: - Only I will take that glory. You, little nit, stay where you are. I'm the best, me… only me…
- Do you want to come with me to the inspector's office to look through those files there, and see if we can find any clues?
- Come on, Denis, list everything and bring it to me. I have a lot of work to do here. We will solve it together when we gather the material. - he said, thinking to himself: - You, kid, will finish everything

and bring it to my hands, and then I will kick you like a ball.

XII

It's been two days. It's Tuesday. The day I met the Cop in the garage. I wake up early and, unlike my usual Tuesday, I'm in a good mood. I will bury this momentary despair deep in the past. I spend the whole morning with my old Ma tidying up the apartment and going shopping. And she is noticeably in a better mood. She believes that I found a girl 'when I became diligent', and I keep silent, seem mysterious and thereby further confirm her suspicion. The Cop doesn't answer until 11:50. Lately he's been calling me later and later, I can sense how irrelevant I'm becoming to him. I kiss the old Ma on the head and cheerfully go to the garage.

- Hello, Peter, I answer the Cop at the entrance to the garage and go in first, and he waits a bit and follows me in so that we don't catch the eyes of passers-by and neighbours.
- Is there anything new, Dominik?

- Nothing for now, I say. There's some buzz going around about some drug, but I haven't looked into it properly yet. I will have information by the next meeting - I'm lying. There was no incitement, nor am I going to gather information about it. It is true that the previous week I had been busy studying Fatih's character and thinking of ways to get closer to the Arabs through him.

- Okay, you can go. - replied to the Cop coldly: - I am satisfied with what you informed me last week.

Well, of course he's pleased. I heard from old Tony that he was talking about how they offered him the position of senior inspector. Those dealers were dangerous, because I gave them to him last time. The only important thing for the slob is to wave his badge around and convince himself that he is someone and something, when no one else notices him.

- All right, Peter. See you next week. - I say. I go outside and wait for him to come out and leave, then I go back to the garage because I heard that the Arabs have started unloading goods into the garage shelter.

As soon as I saw the Cop's back, I went back to sit on the garage steps to smoke. I listen carefully, I expect the

Arabs to leave and that Fatih will stay to seek pleasure in the limelight. That's how it happens. As soon as they leave, he settles down on the boxes and rolls marijuana. As if by chance I found myself in the passage and just as by chance I made myself clumsy, so I tripped over some boxes and made a noise, and he greeted me first.

- Oh, hi, Dominik. Did you just get up, so you're getting wet?

- Well, I didn't, but... sorry, I didn't greet you - How are you? - I say to him like the English: 'How do you do' in passing, and I don't expect an answer. And then I continued: - I looked behind me to check if everything was in place. I thought I heard someone. You know there are a lot of thieves here. I would advise you to keep an eye on things.

- Really? - he found himself in awe, and on his face, I read sincere gratitude for having warned him: - I didn't know that, he says: - You told me well. My bro would immediately blame me if something went wrong. I have to convey to him to better secure the goods. Do you want a smoke? - he offers me a lighter.

- Of course, I immediately accepted and sat next to him.

I liked the Bosnian from the start. With him the conversation somehow flows as if we have always known each other. This makes the situation easier for me, it will be easier for me to reach the Arabs.

- And who told you about those thieves, man? - he asks.

- I saw them a couple of times with my own eyes. The neighbours also talk, old Tony knows everything.

- Have you ever been robbed?

- They didn't, but somebody stole all the equipment from my neighbour, Joanne's, hairdressing salon, and only when did the poor woman collect enough money to open something of her own and have her own business. They also say that she took half of it on credit, and that her boyfriend lent her the rest, and now they've had a fight, it couldn't be worse, my friend. A complete tragedy

- And the cops?

- Didn't arrest them.
- Well, I can't do anything to them. They get caught sometimes, a little detention, but these skilled ones steal to make up for it while you say 'biscuit'.

I can see that he is startled, and he believes everything. He looks at me like I'm Jesus.

- Don't worry, I tell him: - just warn yours, and I'll pay a little more attention to your things when I'm here.
- Thank you, bro. I have to go now, he says: I'm in a hurry to help my bro. See you.

I look after him as he leaves and smile with satisfaction. The first step is successful, I have a green light and an open door. Now, I just need to try not to blow anything. The rest will come by itself.

XIII

- The general secretary of the Croatian Football Association stated that, in the future he will try to prevent the introduction of pyrotechnic devices into the stands.

I sit in the armchair the next morning and listen to the news. I'm glad I made contact with Fatih, but I still have no idea how to get away from the Cop. I honestly didn't even come to my senses when my phone vibrated on my desk. It was Peter. Will that fat man ever leave me alone?

- Hello, kid, where are you?
- At home, Peter.
- Enjoy doing nothing as usual, huh?
- Why do you care what I do?
- I don't… listen now, what kind of riot was that at the game last night? You didn't know anything in advance, did you?
- I didn't. I swear.
- Okay, try to be more knowledgeable next time. See you on Tuesday at twelve. Clear?
- Sure, Peter.

Uh, but it's tiring. Actually, I heard that the Torcida fans were making a fuss as usual, but I was busy looking for information about the Bosnian these days, so I really hated to deal with it. And I see that the Cop will not leave me alone.

I poke around dark web forums as Anonymous. I come across an argument between two fans, so I get involved and stoke the fire.

"Bro, are you stupid or just don't want to understand?"

"ŠTICO, hey, everything on your list, for everything you do and what you've been doing..." - I interjected.

"Hello, Anonymous, on Friday Torcida will fry you..."

That's how little by little I came to the information about who will make a mess at the game on Friday. I had information for the Cop on Tuesday.

Some guys from the region joined the fan group and sold themselves for pittance. At this time, fans were bought and sold rather lightly, everyone would fuck each other for a nickel.

I snitched on the three of them to the Cop. He will spend up to forty-eight hours in custody and nothing to anyone. A little beating over their backs will save my head.

I feel so miserable. I realize that I'm no better than that slob, Peter, maybe I just pretend a little better. I have to get away from him forever, before we become symbiotic forever. What a horror, he dragged me into all this so much that sometimes, when I look in the mirror, it seems to me that I start to look like him physically. God, I'm going crazy...

XIV

After a few days, I met Fatih in a local tavern where everyone from the area gathers and follows the matches. The atmosphere was very heated. Our team, Dinamo Zagreb, was playing and we all cheered fervently. I would say, that evening, they played like they never played before. The team had a successful offence and very dynamic actions. Fatih and I started drunkenly toasting each other and ordered more beer. That's how we got closer and got into a conversation when the match ended.

- My old man was a soccer legend in the 80's. I'm really carried by this atmosphere, I told him while the chanting of satisfied fans was still going on.

- Really? I really like football. I used to play. Now I'm just drooling, so I don't make it, and cigarettes keep me from running, he said.

- Me too, although I've never been a pro, but I've always been an ardent Dinamo fan.

- I supported FC Željezničar from Sarajevo, but now that I'm here, I can join you. And you say, your old man was a legend in the eighties? Man, I'm speechless.

- Yes, yes, I say: - that's how I spent my time at matches cheering him on from a young age. At first, my old lady went too, and then... - I fell silent because I was embarrassed to talk about my family in front of someone I barely know.

- What happened? - he inquired.
- Uh nothing. - I waved my hand.
- What, they didn't agree, did they? Well, what does it matter - it's not your fault.
- Well, you know, quarrels started between them, the old man was prone to fraud. She hid it from me, and when I found out, he had already finished his career. Otherwise, I would probably hate football.
- You don't need to hate anyone or anything. People disagree, it happens. It's all natural. My old man is not a fan of football or sports in general, but I always liked to play and go to matches with my friends in the neighbourhood. And my relatives on my mother's side really like football.

It's not like I can love an old man when he's an asshole, I thought to myself, but I didn't want to talk about it with a stranger. Instead, I continued with the casual conversation.

- Your mother is Bosnian, right?

- Yes, Dad came there on business, he opened a shop. She was looking for a job, then she got a job with him and little by little, I was born and that's how they stayed together.
- You're a very interesting character, Fatih.
- You are ready for me too. We almost moved here. I don't know anyone, can you introduce me to your friends?
- Of course. Come! - I was happy because I became dear to him too. Everything is going according to plan; I am slowly approaching the Arabs.

I took him to the table in the corner where three of my friends were still sitting, all fellow fans of FC Dinamo.

- Luka, Dario, Ivan, this is Fatih, he comes from Bosnia.
- Welcome, Fatih! - the group, already under the influence of alcohol, gladly accepted him.
- And why did you move here? - Dario was curious.
- For work. Here, Dad opens up a space for me with pool tables, gaming machines and a betting shop.
- Ooo… nice, replied Dario. And where did he come from? Where did he get so much money?

Fatih was not offended by this open question. His father had acquired property honestly, and he was not uncomfortable talking about their business activities.

- He came here from Syria, he is engaged in trade, he opened a company there in Bosnia, he met my old Ma and that's how he started his business, now it's expanding.
- And he's an Arab, right? - asked Luka.

Fatih nodded affirmatively: - Yes.

- A successful businessman means?! - Dario asked more rhetorically, then slapped Fatih on the shoulder in such a hearty way: - Come on, let's toast to our new friend and to his business, he said and raised the glass, and then we all put our hands over Fatih's shoulders and poured beer on ex.

From that evening forward, Fatih and I continued our daily socialising, and we often watched matches with my friends in the pub.

XV

As time went on, we became closer. We even started going to matches together. I managed to win him over and he became a true Dinamo fan. Just as if Croatia was his native country. He cheered so fervently; he would stand on the other side only when they played FC Željezničar. I would joke with him about what would happen if Željezničar played against Syria, and he would say that a mother is still a mother. - Be careful, it can offend your old man, don't leave you without a slag, I would tease him.

- He knows that. My father values my mother above all else, and he is not interested in sports, and basically, he renounced Syria, when he took Bosnian citizenship. Now he lives very quietly in Bosnia, he used to say: - My half-brother Adin took over all the work. I work with him. We don't get along very well, but that's a long story.

One day he invited me to his half-brother's newly opened playhouse, which he opened with his business partners from Syria.

- Dominik, I am very happy here with you. I feel like I'm at home. You know I didn't have anyone when I came. You know, Adin opened a playroom today, you remember I told you that he was planning to do that. Do you want to go have a drink and play a game? We can also bet on Dinamo-Hajduk tonight, right?

- Oh, yes... very happy, Fatih. Shall we now? I mean, the game is at eight, and now it's already five. The ticket should be paid at least two hours before the match. Is it far?
- Immediately, painful, but what. It is not far, in the street parallel to the one where Šula's tavern is.

I was amazed when I walked in. It was a fully equipped modern game room, with slot machines, a dart machine, foosball tables. There was also a betting section on the right and everything could be done via computers that were available on several tables in front of the main desk.

- Adin plans to expand this further, just until it gets going. The games will have whatever you desire, even those games where you fight with a virtual opponent and have to use your body. - said Fatih proudly.

That Arab is lying on the money, I thought to myself.

- Let's sit down and drink a beer while we fill out the ticket, he suggested, and I gladly accepted.

The casino was painted light green, with a slightly darker shade bordering around the edges, and a dark blue carpet on the floor. There were more than twenty tables for gamblers and addicts alike, almost all of them full. The poor were looking for a way to make some quick money, and then they mostly fell into even greater misery.

We sat down at a table in the central part, from where the whole room could be seen. Fatih was obviously known by everyone there. Some waved to him from the neighbouring tables, others got up and passed by to answer, while others noticed him already from the door and greeted him warmly. It was obvious that he was well regarded. We bet on Dinamo, of course.

- You are lucky to have such a father. This one of mine lives only his own life, he doesn't care about me, except when he gives me lessons, I confided in him.

- But why, Dominik? You are a young man out of place. I can see that they appreciate you in the end. It is not your fault that there is general unemployment in the country.

- Tell that to my old man…

My head was constantly spinning about how to solve my status as an informant. I need to relax a bit. Everything is going according to plan. I am closer to the Arabs than ever. I don't have to, at least for the few hours I'm here, think about how to get rid of the Cop.

We filled out the slip, and then we played a few games of darts.

- Do you want to play some billiards now? suggested Fatih.

At that moment I saw one of the Arabs approaching us.

- Hey, here's Adin.

- You guys enjoying yourselves?

- Yes, bro, it's the best.

- It is really beautiful, everything is modern, I added.

- This is my half-bro, Adin, and this is Dominik. Remember I told you about him? - Fatih introduced us.

- Yes, yes... that's the nice young man who takes you everywhere and makes you feel at home here, concluded the Arab.

They still think I'm nice. Lucky me. These are mine, just to figure out how to get me out of the jaws of the Cop's blackmail and all the things I've gotten myself into.

- Whatever you need, I'm here, just so you know. I'm going now. I have work waiting for me. Enjoy, you two. And remember, Fatih, after midnight.

The guys are arriving with the goods, we need to place them in the warehouse.

- Thank you, sir, I told him. A man, when he sees me so well-dressed and with manners, would never suspect what I do for a living. One would say 'a young man by example'.
- Bro, actually Dominik is looking for a job.
- So, what are you talking about, Fatih? Such a polished young man, he must be a civil servant. We'll see. I'm in a hurry now.

I was speechless for a moment. I don't believe they made me like that.

- Bro, thank you. Really, I appreciate that you stand up for me so much.
- You're welcome. If we can do something for you, why not help?

We hung around until right before the match began, then headed to the tavern, where the regulars were sitting in front of the large LCD TV and cheering.

When the group parted after the match, the two of us stayed a little longer, and then Fatih had to go help the Arab unloading the goods.

I saw that I had won him over, so I decided to use that evening to get under his skin a little more.

- I'll help you. I have no obligations, I lied. I barely had enough to buy coffee and weed, but I decided to get my freedom even at the cost of several months of sleeplessness.
- Well, come on. If I don't torture you, it's nicer in company.

When we arrived, his half-brother was waiting for the van outside the garage.

- Adin, Dominik came to help us.
- OMG Fatih, don't torture the man here. He is not your carrier. To hold some offices, then to hire him...
- Oh, sir, I didn't come to be hired. I have a little extra time, so I should meet Fatih, just for the sake of socialising.
- Well, come on then. You are such a hard-working young man and I only want you to work on betting tickets for me, I have nowhere else to go.
- That's really nice of you. You know, I don't really choose now.
- Then, consider yourself accepted. You work tomorrow at 2:00 p.m., so we'll see.

I helped Fatih to unload the goods and afterwards each of us went home. I was a little ashamed of myself for using that Bosnian for my own ends, but Machiavellianism prevailed in me. I longed for freedom so much that I would have reached the ninth circle of hell. My mind was so clouded by the pressure that I aspired to surpass Raskolnikov and a dead greengrocer.

XVI

The next day I went to the game room, as we agreed. The work was not difficult, and I liked to take my mind off my problems. So far, they haven't registered me, I'm already working part-time illegally.

I started to pray to God again. It was really nice when I went to church with my folks as a kid, when they were still together and loved each other. I felt so safe then. Everything was nice and simple. I didn't have to worry about anything, they took care of me. My duty was just to enjoy life, socialize and play sports. It seemed to me that life was uncomplicated and ran smoothly. I know now that my family had problems then, like everyone else, but somehow everything was easier: they were both financially well-off, employed, and provided with a roof over their head. They did not, like us, have to live, or rather - they survive from today to tomorrow. For the most part, most of them could be sure that their first job would pay them what they wanted and where they wanted, and that they would probably receive their pension where they got a job; they travelled, shopped, dressed nicely, ate in restaurants... Today, if I wasn't old, I would turn into bread and pâté. That poor thing always digs up something from somewhere and devises a plan to mix anything in with me, take it out of her mouth, and that's why this current situation of mine shakes me even more.

Thoughts were running through my head like that, until someone pulled me out of them to ask me something. This is how I automatically printed the electronically registered slips and mechanically handed them to the users with the robotically pronounced "Please" and the drawn smile learned in my many years of career as an office clerk.

- Excuse me, can I have one ticket?
- Yes, of course, I offered what was requested without noticing that Fatih was standing in front of me, head and chin.
- Hey, man, you got it right.

Only then did I come to my senses and realize that it was him.

- Oh, Fatih, sorry. I'm really sorry.
- Relax. A lot of people pass by here, if you could look at all their faces and remember them, you'd go crazy... But, do you want to take a walk after your shift?
- I will, of course, I would like to, just so you know.

Around midnight we went out for a walk around the area, but after less than ten minutes we were caught by a terrible rain accompanied by a storm and lightning strikes. We barely managed to escape under the terrace of the building. We decided to wait a bit because we thought it would pass quickly, so we could continue walking, but the whole time it was pouring like a river, and it didn't seem like it would stop anytime soon.

Then Fatih suggested that we move to the garage shelter.

That's how the story started, when Fatih opened the envelope and went to arrange the cake. Put together a couple of joints. He took out a grass stump and offered me one, which I gladly accepted.

We stayed in the garage shelter until before dawn. We were so high that we got into a terrible trip: Fatih pretended to be a stand-up comedian, climbed up on the pallets, then cracked jokes, while I threw them from below 'from the audience'.

- Do you know the name of the garden through which the big mouth passes? - he called out to the imaginary audience.
- Hahaha... I'm already laughing like crazy.
- Shut up there. Why are you laughing like a deaf pig?
- Hahaha... I burst into even stronger giggles.
- It's not hahaha… it's not, boy, that's the wrong answer… the garden that the big mouth goes through may have been thick at one time…

I was already in tears from uncontrollable laughter.

- And now it's rare, isn't it? - I don't stop grinning.
- Desolate, hollow-headed, desolate... you don't know the rhyme. Deserted as a desert... and camels walk on it.
- Hahahaha... I was holding my stomach and rolling on the floor.
- Listen to you below, you, you who are grinning, he pointed at me: - Come upstairs, well, now you are going to perform, he said dead seriously.

I went upstairs, shaking like a rod. I think it's real, and from those bags around it seems to me that it's security, so I can't move away and my brain immediately starts working like clockwork:

- Who always faithfully waits for his wife at home?
- Loverboy, lover boy - he shouted and waved some rag he found there.
- Well, it's not, but so are the courts.
- Hahaha… he was giggling until he passed out.

When the initial madness subsided a little, we sat down next to each other and smoked pot in peace, only letting out a few good fora from time to time.

- You are very good at this focus, Bosnian. If you have any more of these, I can hook you up with a dealer here in the neighbourhood. It pays well, that's all. - I'm kidding a bit because I'm pretty dazed from the weed, but partly I want to test the Bosnian because I want to know more about those Arabs.
- He finds himself barely able to speak from the intoxicated. I can see that he would say something else to me, but he doesn't have the strength or is waiting for a more favourable moment.

I'm not quite myself either, and my experience as an informant has taught me that I should be silent, the cat alone comes to the doorman.

XVII

The next morning, I woke up around noon. I barely remember anything from the previous evening, it seemed more like a dream. The old Ma went out. I don't skip my daily practice of staring at the ceiling and running frantic thoughts through my head to get out of the state I've fallen into. The fact that I got a job in a betting shop will not save me. On the contrary, the Cop may think that I now know even more about local criminals because I have even more contact with people and can hear things in passing, so he could be even more on my neck. I silently pray Our Fathers and Hail Marys on repeat. Those are the only two prayers I know.

Since there is still plenty of free time until my shift, I decided to go to church. It beats laying down and lamenting my fate. The childhood memory of that place gave me hope that, if I were to go, I'dl find peace and deliverance from the mire in which I have been sinking deeper and deeper into lately.

I don't know why I stopped going to church, it was close, only a five-minute walk away. I suppose I was ashamed before God, I simply forgot that everyone is given the opportunity to atone for their sins.

I stopped at the entrance and took a deep breath. I asked for forgiveness in advance; for entering this sanctuary in such a fallen state in the first place and for the years I spent neglecting God. I proceeded to cross myself, kissed the statue at the entrance on the left, and entered. Inside, I saw an old friend from school selling candles. I bowed my head to sneak past her. I was a promising, young man, worthy of all praise among the teachers at school. I was so consumed by shame; I wouldn't know how to tell her I amounted to nothing.

Unfortunately for me, she recognized me.

- Dominik, is that you? - All beaming came out in front of me.

I tried to pretend that I didn't hear her, that it wasn't me, but it was in vain, she was already too close and she could see in my eyes that it was me. I think she had a thing for me back in the day.

- Hey, hi, Christine, I can barely speak.

- Where've you been? - She continued, equally energetic and smiling. - Come and let me hug you, I haven't seen you in a hundred years.

Reluctantly, I held out my hands to her, aware that a close hug leads to a close conversation, and I was not mentally prepared for any of that.

- So, what are you doing? Where do you live?
- I've been abroad for a while. - I lied.
- Really? Where?
- In Germany.
- Really? And what were you doing there?
- Some office work. - I continued and I just started to be convinced of the truth of my fabrications: - And you? Where did you come from? Are you married?
- Ah, there - she lowered her head, and I could see that she was uncomfortable talking: - so, there was a vacancy and I applied, what I am going to do, I have to do something.
- So, are you married? Do you have a family?
- Oh, I don't have, I don't have...

I saw that now she would start avoiding me, so I was relieved.

- Nice, Christine. Sorry, I came to light a candle, so I have to go to work, my shift starts soon.

- No problem, Dominik, stop by again. - she shyly looked at me under her eyebrows and I saw that she still liked me. She was still very pretty. I wish I could pull myself out of this and ask her out.

Well, Christine, you took my mind off my troubles. I lit the candle, turned once more to say goodbye and left. I wasn't sure if I would visit the church again anytime soon. As much as I wanted to, I was ashamed and embarrassed before both God and, now, Christine.

XV

Like before, the time at the casino passed quickly. While on the clock, I could follow the games, and it raised my adrenaline a bit to help me work. However, my mind would still wonder… Should I try church again tomorrow? Is Christine always on the same shift? Maybe I should learn another prayer first. Where is Ma's prayer book? I should go to Mass. I'm going to learn this... I'm ashamed of that... Christine is hot... How do I lose the Cop?

The shadow of that bald man hung over my sky and made every moment dark. In the Arabs, I saw a glimmer of light that could dissipate the storm that's been ravaging my being for four years.

When I finished my work, the Bosnian was waiting for me outside.

- Hi, Dominik. I was passing through and thought we'd take a walk around the area, if you want.
- Sure, Fatih.

It seems that he really accepted me. That's good.

We made a couple of laps by the end, and then the thirst kicked in:

- How about I get us some beer, and we can hang out in the garage? It looks like it's going to rain again.
- Great idea. - he replied.

We were sitting on the boxes like before, drinking beer and spitting, when the Bosnian suddenly took out his beer again to stack it.

- Take it, he tells me.

I take it without saying a word. I don't know where he got so much weed from, but that doesn't even matter at this point. It will help me relax and put the Cop out of my mind at least for a while.

That's how we got into the story. Time flies. We don't even notice.

At one point, Fatih tells me in confidence that his cousin in Bosnia runs a marijuana plantation.

- And that's why you're so popular? And I really wondered how it is that you always have it, but I say to myself, you have money, so it comes to you as a 'good day'.

- Well, I only do that when I'm there. Here you can always get as little as you need somewhere, especially when you deal with trade and forwarding. But you said that you can find me a dealer here? - he remembered what I told him last time, and I was kidding. I don't know where I'm going now.

This is the ticket to get closer to Arabs and get out of here, I think. It's a big mouthful, but I must swallow if I think I'm going to get out of this shit.

- Well, you know, I could find buyers for that cousin of yours here.

- Really? Where?

- I will give you all the details soon. - He seems to be taken with this idea: - Just check with that cousin if he is interested, I say, and I have no idea how I'm going to solve it, but I decide to get into the game, so as they play, that's how I'll play. Bluffing has become my professional deformation anyway. By tomorrow he will forget about it, if only I will investigate those Arabs now.

XVIII

I arrived at work a little earlier, so I decided to fill out a slip and smoke a cigarette. For the last four years, since I've been under the paw of the Cop, I've been my own best company. I'm too depressed and distracted, I'm not my old self anymore. The only thing I can still enjoy is going to those matches with my friends, I am truly relaxed there.

"Agency for support of information systems and information technologies denies Karamarko, the reaction of the state election commission is awaited: "There was no mandate theft, no one even complained ".
"The spectre of the alleged theft of mandate: A lot of noise from nothing"
"Survey: Citizens assessed: The new government is completely unsuccessful, and the main culprit is -

Orešković" - the news from the radio is tearing my brain apart. Is it possible that people still listen to this and believe that a change of government will bring betterment to this country? It won't work for me anyway if I don't get rid of the Cop, and he stays where he is, whether the government changes or not. - Focus, focus, I'm trying to calm myself down and concentrate: - you have to think about the problem, leave the political situation and people behind. How will you keep your reputation?

- Hi, Dominik! So early? - Fatih appeared, suddenly, and took me out of my thoughts.
- Yeah. I'm a little early. Until I get a foothold, you know, to learn a little from the side-lines.
- Come on, don't be a nerd, he was teasing me: - Do we want to watch the game tomorrow in the pub, and then a joint at our place?
- Sure. I finish work early tomorrow.
- I want to ask you something in confidence, he whispered to me: - Don't let me down.
- Don't worry, Fatih. I won't. - I said.
- Great, he replied cheerfully, turned on his heel and left.

The whole day I was thinking about what he wanted to know. It occurred to me that it could be about selling pot. I wouldn't know what to do if it was, so I tried to get it out of my mind. Hopefully he already had forgotten it, I told myself. I was afraid that if I continued the lie I had fallen into, I would get hurt on both sides.

My shift went by quickly, I did things mechanically, my head was a little easier while my hands were busy.

- my head was spinning, as I walked like a robot along the street towards my apartment. I entered quietly so as not to awake my mom, hung my jacket on the hanger in the hallway, took off my tennis shoes, standing on the heel of the other foot, and kicked them into a corner down the hall. I took off my suit and threw it over a chair in the room. I didn't feel like taking a shower, but I smelled of smoke and sweat, so I did anyway. The old girl would faint if she saw me in bed like that. The water felt amazing on my body, but I didn't have to shower for very long. It seemed to me that a part of the burden pressing down on me was washed away from my head.

I couldn't sleep for a long time, I was thinking about the Cop, my life, and the old Ma... Where is that prayer book? I'd better look for it tomorrow. I wouldn't want to wake her up.

XIX

The next day, the alarm woke me up at nine. I had to get ready for work at ten that day.

I lazily rubbed my eyes and barely got up to put the water on the stove. It was Friday, so the old Ma went to the market. She always got up early on Fridays and went out to find fresh food at the best possible prices, which she sparingly distributes over the week. I loved her, so it was easier for me that she was not here. It's hard for me to look her in the eyes, I don't know how much longer I can lie to her. On the table there were still warm fried bacon, cheese, and cream. She always left me a little something before she went out.

What will Fatih ask me tonight? ... Where is that prayer book? ... How to get rid of the Cop? - the thoughts kept oppressing me. I rummaged through the shelves and drawers of the apartment looking for that prayer book. Suddenly, I smelled something strange. Fuck, coffee! I ran to the kitchen, the water had already boiled, and the kettle had started to burn. I quickly turned the stove off, pushed the kettle into the sink and poured cold water over it. I was just about to set the apartment on fire.

- Jesus Christ, I cursed out loud: - I should pray to God for a little more intelligence.

It's twenty to ten. I have no more time to waste. I gave up looking for the book. I ate the two cream puffs and grabbed a couple more and some cheese for the road. The coffee will be missed.

It's raining again; I was all wet by the time I got to the Casino. I had to get dry with one of the heaters there. Time passed rather slowly today. Before noon, people visit these places less often. Somehow, I managed to make it to 6:00 pm.

Fatih and an umbrella were waiting for me out front.

- Come on, the match is about to start.

- Thank you for waiting for me. I got absolutely soaked today.

I saw that Fatih was in an unusually good mood. The whole day I was haunted by the mysterious subject of this inquiry, and that it could be decisive for me to end this chapter of my life and start a new one in which I will not be ashamed to be the main character of.

We drank a lot at the pub and toasted each other every hour as if we were at some kind of wedding, as if we were really starting a new life.

- Dominik, to Dinamo and Željezničar!
- Ha ha, Fatih, I accept only because you put Dinamo first!
- Oh, don't do that. If you came to my place in Bosnia, you too would fall in love with Sarajevo without even noticing.
- Be that as it may, we are here now. - I teased.

It wouldn't be long before one of us would raise a toast again.

- To you, Fatih, my new friend!
- To us, bro! To life!
- And to girls! - I said, and Christine's image was vividly drawn in my mind. God, why am I thinking about that girl so much?

And so, it went on endlessly until the local bar "Šula" had to close the bar, sometime around midnight, and he literally had to throw us out as we were drunk.

The fresh air woke us up a little, and we got up with our elbows on each other and walked around in a circle for half an hour when the rain caught up with us again and gave us a good shower.

- Now I'm dripping like I've come out of a river, Fatih laughed loudly.
- Do you want me to roll up your sleeve a bit to help you dry off? Hahaha! - I continued.
- Just no violence, please. Here, you can see that I'm shaking like a stick... hahaha... Hey, Dominik, I don't feel like going home. Do you want us to roll up a joint each?
- How can I refuse you? - I was kidding. I didn't feel like going home either. On top of that, I had the next day off. I wanted to be honest enough to sleep through the night tomorrow and not think about the Cop.

XX

We enter the garage and sit on the boxes, just like the previous times. The Bosnian automatically rolls the joint. I'm sitting with my legs crossed and I'm twirling the thread that has come off the lower part of my jeans leg. I have to treat my nerves with something until the weed starts working.

If the old Ma saw me, she would scream. This has become a practice for me, I could get hooked. Even if she knew where I work, she still wouldn't be right. And Christine would be disappointed too. Then again, anything is better than the Cop's paws. He would chain me like a slave for a year if I allowed myself to surrender to him now. How to get rid of him?

- Hey… wake up. - Fatih waved his hand in front of my eyes. It seems I was lost in thought: - Where have you wandered off to?
- Well, I'm sorry, Fatih, I thought a little.
- I see that you are who knows where. Hold on... And if it's not some girl in question, aaa...? - he sat next to me and nudged me with his elbow.
- Well, er… actually…
- And it is, it is! - he rejoiced: - Who is she? Speak!
- Well... - I decided to tell him about Christine, it's better to tell him that, than to let him continue to squeeze me about what I'm thinking about... about the motherfucking cop - Well, you know - there is one girl I like...
- Well, who is she? Do I know her?
- Well, I do not know. Maybe. That's my friend from high school... and I liked her then...
- So, where did you find her now?
- Well, you know, she works at the church.

- Oh fuck… I guess she's a good girl, if you've liked
  her for so long…
- Well, she is.
- And where was she until now... what happened
  since high school?
- I do not know. I haven't seen her.
- Well, bro, why don't you ask her out for a drink?
  Ask her about her interests.
- I will. - I say.

We talked like that for a long time. Every few minutes I
would wonder what he wanted to ask me, and finally I
concluded that he just wanted to win me over so that we
would mingle together because there is no company
here. It wasn't long after my conclusion, when the
Bosnian suddenly became serious:

- Dominik... um, you know... I told you I had
  something to ask you tonight, in confidence,
  remember?

It cut through me like a cold shower. I didn't expect this.

- Errr, yes… I remember… What's the matter?
- By the way... do you have a dealer?
- I have, bro, I just haven't seen him yet. We'll sort
  it out. Is your cousin willing?
- He wants to see the offer first.

- Look, bro, I'll see with him, then I'll let you know, but I should see the goods first.
- You don't have to worry about that. We will go to Bosnia in my van, to see the plantation.
- Deal. I'll get back to you these days while I talk to the dealer.
- Look, he is looking for a good buyer in Croatia. See that he is reliable and pays well. - emphasized the Bosnian.
- Fatih my bro, don't worry, everything is checked, I say.
- Good. You survey the situation and see if anything needs to be resolved, then we'll come to an agreement. - he said with satisfaction and patted me on the shoulder.

There is a God after all. This could be the answer to my prayers to get out of debt slavery. Still, it seems that going to church was worth it... for several reasons, I smiled contentedly inside myself... I really should look for that prayer book...

XXI

I waited a few days to call Fatih to tell him, of course, a fictional story. I phoned him on after my shift on Friday:

- Hello, bro! What are you doing?
- Well, hi, Dominik, he was happy when he heard me: - Do you have any news for me?
- There is something, I try to be discreet. Can you come and take a walk?
- Of course, just to put something on and I'll arrive. I'll be there in five minutes.
- See you then, I said.

The Bosnian arrived at the speed of light. We all know how to be quick when we need to fill our pockets. Well, soon mine will be full too. I've swallowed a lot of shit with the Cop these four years, I can hold on a little longer, and I will finally be free. I didn't believe that one joke would get me this far.

- Hey, I'm here. - the Bosnian greeted cheerfully: - Where are we going?

It was already midnight, and it was a beautiful and pleasant summer evening, perhaps the neighbourhood park.

- Fatih; there should be a bench under an oak tree in the most secluded part where the light from a streetlamp could not reach. We won't be noticed there.

- Shall we go to the park?

- Yes, the Bosnian immediately accepted.

We walked quite fast and kept quiet the whole three minutes it took to get to our destination. When we sat down, Fatih asked:

- And?

- Look, I told you before that I know a guy who is interested in the job and I met him the day before yesterday.

- And? And? - the Bosnian was impatient.

- And he's interested, very much so. - I lied, and I'm so deep in that lie that I'm starting to believe it: - And, listen, Fatih, he's asking for samples and strict discretion, so everything would go through me... and the payment too.

- Excellent. That suits me just fine as well, Fatih agreed.

- Then everything is settled as far as work is concerned. Just to see the goods.

- On Sunday, the old pa should be bringing something in from Bosnia. You will go with me and in the meantime, we will stop by my cousin's place so you can see the plantation and make arrangements. Deal! - he offered me his fist, smiling.

- We shake hands. - I heartily accepted.

We spent some more time in the park smoking without saying a word. Each one assembled his own film in his head based on the story he believed in. Then we got up just like that, bid each other farewell with a strong handshake, a hug with a pat on the back, and parted ways.

XXII

I couldn't sleep that night. I was fitting the pieces of the puzzle into my story of freedom and thinking about how to fit the Cop into it so that when it suited me, I could remove him with ease. Until now, I haven't mentioned anything to him about Bosnians and Arabs, fearing that he might ruin my plan, but now I think it's time to tell him something, that is, I agree, so that I can continue with my game. After constant thinking and rethinking, in the morning I make the final decision to call him:

- Yes? - his irritated voice was heard on the other side of the line. Sounds like I woke him up.

- Hello, Peter. - I said almost shyly.

- What do you want, Dominik? Is it something so urgent that you call me at seven in the morning?

- Well, hey, I met those Arabs, you know, and I'm a bit suspicious of them... not over the phone though.

- Okay, meet me at ten, you know where. - he lowered the sharpness of his voice a little, but it was still clear that he was angry that I called him so early, when he was drinking his first morning coffee, alone in the office. He didn't wait for me to say anything else. He abruptly ended the call.

I had no choice but to wait for ten and until then prayed my two prayers. The old Ma was not at home. She must have gone over to her neighbour's house for morning coffee. Maybe I could have gone to the church. Now I have enough money. I could buy that prayer book... maybe buy something for the Mum... and what if Christine sees me? What should I tell her? Maybe I'd better not go... but I'd still like to see her. I think I'll go anyway. I put on my jacket and headed towards the church.

XXIII

After the conversation with Dominik, Peter was already rubbing his palms with satisfaction. This smelled like success, the fulfilment of his greedy desires, he was only one step away from being Senior Inspector. Those Arabs smell like a big bite that is just big enough to take that step and leave Denis wallowing in the mud of failure and misery.

He tapped his foot as he sorted out some papers and waited for the breakfast break to meet up with Dominik. Everything had to be kept in strict secrecy so that no one would take away even a tiny crumb of his glory.

At half past 9 there was a knock on his office door. Who is that now? - he wondered. He thought about pretending he wasn't there, but he was afraid the Senior Inspector would be looking for him, so he couldn't bring himself to do it. He was silent for moment, coughed, and, as if preoccupied, in a voice ask:

-   Who is it?
-   It's Denis. Can I come in?

That louse again. What does he want? - thought Peter: I would prefer to slap him, and I can't. I have to be kind. What does everyone see in that troublemaker?

- Come in, but please be brief. I am busy.
- Well, actually, I wanted to invite you to come to breakfast with us. A new bakery opened close the police station. Their potato pie is excellent.
- Very nice of you, Denis, but I can't today. I have to go pay some bills and finish up some other things in town.
- Well, if you want, I can buy us a pie and we can finish it together, Denis suggested.

Peter was already boiling inside, it seemed that lava was coming out of his ears. Why is this prick always so nice? Calm down, Peter, he told himself, count to ten, breathe...

- Listen, Denis, I'm in a hurry, really. Some other time, thank you. And then he buried his nose in the papers to let Denis know that the conversation was over.

Denis understood and left the office.

XXIV

356. 357. 358... I counted the steps to the church: - Today was a very nice day... I'm going to buy a prayer book; Two more hours until I meet the Cop... I'm in a dangerous circle now... Can I swallow this big morsel? What would I do if the Arabs should discover me? I could be crushed from all sides... This doesn't make sense anymore. I have to put an end to this. Then I will fly free like a bird— 1,232. 1,233 step! I arrive at the church and cross myself... and there she is. As beautiful as ever.

- Hi, Christine! How are you?
- Oh... Hi, Dominik! - she was happy for me, I see. A smile shines on her face: - Ohh... I'm fine, fine. How are you?
- Me?!... I had some free time, so I thought I'd stop by...
- Oh, well... - she shyly lowered her head and looked at the floor.
- Hey, Christine, you wouldn't by any chance have any prayer books lying around, would you? I'd like to buy one.
- Of course! She jumped up and went to look for a prayer book in church shop, happy that she could

direct herself somewhere and put an end to her shyness: - Here, she handed me a small booklet in a brown cardboard cover: - Here you go.

- Wow, thanks! How much?

- Forty-five Kunas.

- Here, take it... keep the rest as a contribution to the church - I said, holding out a fifty Croatian Kuna note.

- Thank you. - she looked down again.

- Christina?

- Yes?

I wanted to ask her out some time, but then I thought that maybe it wouldn't be smart in my situation, I shouldn't involve her in my problems. Her "Yes" was followed by a long dramatic pause, until I finally summoned myself to answer her.

- Hey, I need some rosaries. Do you have those?

- Oh, of course. - she got a little confused, as if she expected me to ask her something else: - What color would you like?

- Red ones. Give me two.

- Here, that's twelve Kuna.

- There you go...er, one's for you.

- Ah, well… thanks… uh why?

- Well, you are very kind and helpful.
- Thank you... - she went silent, and then she whispered: - You too, I love you too.
- I have to go. - I rushed not to mess things up even more. Maybe I shouldn't have gone to church after all.

XXV

Peter left the office at 9;42. He trotted with quick steps and constantly looked back to make sure no one was following him. He was most worried that Denis would accidentally discover him and ruin his chance to be promoted. Even worse than that, it pained him that Denis, or anyone else, could get the title he wanted and therefore be higher, more important, more valuable, and more respected than him.

He went around the block, stopped at the bank to withdraw some money, so that whoever was following him would think he was paying the bills, then went around another corner and when he was sure that no one was following him, he entered the parking garage where he was to meet with Dominik.

XXVI

I tried not to ran out of the church. I was so confused. I walked quickly and never once looked behind me, not even when the rosary I bought in the church fell out of my hand at the church gate, not even when I heard Christine calling me after a while to tell me that I had dropped that rosary, nor when I got splashed by a car that passed me.

When I got to the garage, it was only 9;50. I decided to take a short walk around the end. In the meantime, I got caught in the rain. I was wet to the skin, dirty and dead hungry when I came back to the garage at ten o'clock to meet the Cop.

Peter greeted me at the entrance with a   disgust, and in a big surprise: - For God's sake, Dominik, what do you look like?

- Well, it's raining and i got splashed by a car... so I got a little wet"- I explained.

- Ah... I see... just a little? he smirked, - So the Arabs?

- Peter, listen, this is top secret. I got wet because I followed those Arabs to make sure that everything, I'm about to tell you is correct.

- Speak you fool, immediately - he said commandingly and slapped me.

I had to keep my composure and not let my anger overwhelm me. That cop scumbag! Whenever he got nervous and worried about his ass, he allowed himself to take it out on me: - Take it easy, Peter. You will find out everything. I have to introduce you to the story. - I strove to remain calm and maintain a friendly tone towards him to fully win his trust and be on the right path towards the realisation of my intention.

- Well, come on, talk. - he calmed down a bit when he saw how calm I was.

- You see, the other night I was sitting there outside the garage on the bench smoking weed. It seemed like an evening like any other. So, someone passed by, it was warm, the breeze was blowing...

- Dominik, don't joke with me. Breeze?! Say what's up with the Arabs.

I actually gave myself time to wrap up my story, but I saw that I had to think and act faster.

- I'm telling you, then that van with the Arabs came by and broke the silence. I didn't let it happen like that. I immediately got up and looked for a way to ask who they were and what they were looking for there. They were unloading some big boxes. I watched them from the sidelines. They seemed heavy and there were a lot of them. They were talking about something, writing some codes on the boxes. It immediately looked like a secret language to me.

- What was in the boxes, Dominik?

- You won't believe it: weapons.

- Are you lying?! How did you find out? Did you open the boxes? How?

- Oh, no. I just watched them there that evening. They loaded it into the garage shelter, packed up and left. My attention was drawn to a Bosnian who was with them. He was guarding the goods all the time and then the entrance while they were loading it. I immediately suspected that something big was at stake when they needed insurance. Clothes and spices don't really need a gun to guard them, even in this day and age when everyone is hungry. It immediately dawned on me that I should follow him and find out what it was all about.

- Just a moment, Dominik. I have to report that I am staying on the field, this will take a minute. - said the Cop and took the cell phone: - Hello, Inspector. I apologize if I interrupted anything important. I am on the verge of discovering a great conspiracy and I am staying in the field.

- Okay, Peter - the Inspector's voice was heard from the other side: - Just don't mess this up. Is Denis with you?

- Well, Inspector, I left at the beginning of the breakfast break, it was urgent. He wanted to go to eat pie–

- Pie? - the Senior Inspector Mr Albert was furious.

- Well, yes. - answered Peter innocently.

- Stay as long as necessary, and I'll talk to Denis later - the inspector retorted angrily and abruptly ended the call.

XXVII

Although it seemed to Dominik that Fatih was very attached to him and that he gave him infinite trust, that was not exactly the case. We are living in a crazy time when we all became   half-beasts, and only partially left them to be human, civilized, and empathetic, and in some, this feature was even completely absent. Fatih, just like Dominik, had his own interest in the whole story. When the stew is being cooked, everyone looks to grab a piece of meat, and to other offer leftovers Although he was well-off, Fatih wanted to get as much money out of this business as possible. No, he wasn't driven by greed or avarice, Fatih had another problem. He was his father's favourite child and quite free from obligations, he used to spend time in underground casinos and slot clubs, although wealthy, fell into gambling debts. He had to find a way to solve it.

As soon as he parted ways yesterday with Dominik, he called his cousin and the black sheep of the family, Sakib from Bosnia, to give him a tempting offer and secure as much income for himself in advance as possible.

- Hello, Sakib, I have an offer for you, cuz.

- Is it confidential? - asked Sakib.

- You already know what's going on. I don't have concrete information yet, but he says they must have a man. They need a price to be negotiated and they want to see the goods.

- Not a problem. You know the goods are first class. I want clean diamonds; I won't risk anything else. I already have one offer from Croatia.
- I'm taking care of everything, bro, don't worry, it must be a good catch. This guy really seems interested. Just so you know, I want half of all the earnings.
- Didn't be greedy Fatih? - protested Sakib.
- I assure you I am not. It will be enough for both of us. I smelled good money.
- Okay, you're the boss, but make sure there's enough for you and me.
- Don't question that. Not enough, but too much! Sunday before noon?
- Good. The goods will be ready when you let us know, but an advance payment must be made upon collection.
- Don't worry about it. You know I'm not wrong when it comes to that. Come on, tell me, have I ever let you down, bro?
- You have not, my bro.
- Well, then why are you making drama for no reason? I'll see you on Sunday, okay?
- See you, bro.

XXVIII

I spent almost two hours in the garage with the Cop. He smoked all my fabrications about Bosnians and Arabs. I could also become an actor. The fear of being discovered and the immense desire to finally break free from this years-long slavery to the Cop's assholes made me nimble and very resourceful in every situation. I gained the ability to think ahead and predict everyone's move, I began to know the psychology of people in detail. The Cop became very interested in the Arab group and firmly believed that they were really smuggling weapons. In addition, there he smelled a direct ticket for securing the position of Senior Inspector.

- And how did you get close to the Bosnian? - he asked me, his eyes shining greedily.

- Peter, you know that I have a nose and a skilful hand for that. By the way, this is the modern world. Social networks are enough to find out everything about anyone in advance. I found the Bosnian on Facebook and sent him a request.

- It would be better if you didn't lie to me, Peter was making a stern expression of distrust, and he was smiling to himself like a dog when he smelled the piece of mutton meat intended for him.

- Trust me, Peter, this is the biggest job ever. Just give me a free hand and trust me. It will take me time to research everything in detail.

Peter was watching me squint with those tiny, indented pig eyes under his short eyelashes. His look said "kid, I appreciate you playing a dangerous game, but I smelled a valuable catch, so I'll give you that ounce of time".

- Good, my good Dominik, he said, imitating a paternal voice of tenderness. You have my trust.

He liked to pretend to be a fatfher-figure to me. He would often remind me of how little my negligent father cared for me. My Pa believed in only I made him look and was interested in nothing but his own ass. Smart and well-mannered, just as my mother taught me to be.   She is the only one I wanted to fight for. The Cop's tone caused even more anger in me. I didn't know what kind of strategy I was going to set. I had no idea what exactly I was getting myself into. I felt that I was playing with dangerous players for whom my previous games with the Cop were childish, but also my drive to survive, to get out of the clutches of that old fat pig, to finally feel freedom – the determination was stronger than ever.

- My dear Dominik, daydreaming are we? - the Cop took me out of my thoughts: - You're not hiding something from me, huh?

- Oh, no, that's right. I tell you; I need time to examine everything in detail. I often meet Bosnians, almost every day. I believe I will have more information these days.

- Okay, I won't hold you back any longer. Go and uncover what's going on there as soon as possible. - I saw that he couldn't wait for me to leave so that he could go investigate and search for information himself because he didn't trust me completely.

But that didn't concern me anymore. Let him go and search, he won't be able to find out anything anyway. Now, I need a plan to turn the whole thing to my advantage and get through unscathed.

XXIX

After talking with Sakib, Fatih wiped the sweat from his forehead. He could finally breathe a little. He opened another in a series of threatening messages from acquaintances from whom he borrowed money for gambling:

- Fatih, I hope you haven't forgotten that you owe me rent since the New Year. If it didn't occur to you not to answer me, because I'll send my boys to your door to beat the shit out of you.

He dialled the number from which the message came and confidently addressed the guy on the other end of the mobile connection:

- Dude, I'm sorry for what you've been waiting for. I have some money to give you today. You get the rest by the end of the week.
- Listen fool, I'll forgive you this time and I'll give you until the end of the week, but only because I respect your family, otherwise I'd nail you to a tree to hang like a birdhouse.
- Calm down, please, I give you my word. - Fatih replied calmly.
- No need, but I want the full amount to see on Sunday at seven o'clock in the evening. I'm waiting for you under the oak and don't let me down. Clear?!
- Clear.

- Good. - said the voice on the other side and hung up.

This time, Fatih was hardly shaken by such a conversation. He already had a plan in his head how to deceive Dominik and Sakib, to take the money and go where no one would be able to find him. Then everything will start from the beginning and gambling will be left. He took the cell phone. Just one more ticket, he thought, and played a few games online with a stake of 2,000 Kuna. He then called to update him.

- Dominik, it's Fatih. I was talking to my cousin. On Sunday we go to see the "products".
- That suits me. - answered Dominik shortly, under constant fear that someone might be eavesdropping on him: - You'll pick me up from work tonight so we can agree on everything?
- That's right, said Fatih cheerfully, rubbing his palms and already imagining himself on some tropical beach drinking cocktails.

XXX

After the meeting, Peter hastily went back downtown with the intention of identifying Dominik's Arabs and checking whether they have files in the register.

Happiness is smiling me back; the time has come to Peter shows his quality. And there was time. - he thought as he walked towards the station with big, brisk steps. He was so excited about this case and imagined himself strutting on the pedestal of the highest inspector, looking down on all those petty officials, and especially trampling on Denis, that little sycophant and hypocrite, who ruins his reputation and always jumps in front of him to court superiors. He fantasizes about being appointed chief of police, how everyone bows to him, congratulates him and is a little envious, but also afraid of him, and the girls begin to sigh for him when he goes out for a walk, and he just sits on the terrace of the most expensive cafe on the main street, puts his gun on the table, and slowly sips his coffee, while occasionally looking under his eye at known criminals who are no longer allowed to steal even a penny from him in the store. With the rush of his imagination, his step became more and more brisk, and he waved his arms beside his body so violently that it seemed as if he would catch a flight and soar above the ground. When he reached the station, he was drenched with sweat dripping down his forehead in the middle of his bald head, and his heart was like cannon fire at intervals quite close to a heart attack. At the entrance, he bumped into Denis, whom he did not even greet, and in his haste, he brushed his shoulder so hard that he staggered and almost fell over the threshold. He rushed straight to his office and slammed the door while Denis remained at the entrance dumbfounded and with his mouth open, straightening his wrinkled suit with his hands as he struggled not to fall, dragging himself along the front door when Peter hooked him.

Only when he settled down in the office chair and started the computer, Peter became aware of how strongly his heart was beating and how much he was dripping with sweat. It took him a few minutes to come to his senses and get some air. His shins were burning from walking fast. He entered the electronic criminal records system and as he waited for it to start, he got up to get a glass of water. He drank one while standing, and took the other to drink while he followed possible traces of the transgressions of the newly arrived Arabs. The application ran for a full six minutes until he finally opened the system, and to him it seemed like he was waiting for an eternity. He stomped his foot and snapped his fingers, took a sip of water, and then circled back to the beginning. He had great expectations, like Dicken's hero, but each step in the research left those expectations filled with disappointment and the awareness that they would still have to trust Dominik and share the catch with him. He searched for everything from the back and forth, called his colleagues from Bosnia, but was unable to find anything. When he left the office, it was already deep into the night, in just a few minutes it would strike midnight. The muscles in his legs and arms ached from the brisk walking and flailing that day and he couldn't wait to get in the car and drag himself home to bed. He was covered in sweat, but he didn't care, he collapsed on the bed like a sow in the mud in the warmth of his pigpen and snored the sleep of the righteous. In the morning, they will continue to sniff and question Dominik. in just a few minutes it struck midnight. The muscles in his legs and arms ached from the brisk walking and flailing that day and he couldn't wait to get in the car and drag himself home to bed. He was covered in sweat, but he didn't care, he collapsed on the bed like a sow in the mud in the warmth of his pigpen and snored the sleep of the righteous. In the morning, He will continue to sniff and question Dominik. in just a few minutes it struck midnight. The muscles in his legs and arms ached from the brisk walking and flailing that day and he couldn't wait to get in the car and drag himself home to bed. He was covered in sweat, but he didn't care, he collapsed on the bed like a sow in the mud in the warmth of his pigpen and snored the sleep of the righteous. In the morning, they will continue to sniff and question Dominik.

XXXI

It's Saturday, late afternoon. The end of the shift is approaching. Tomorrow we are going to Bosnia to see the goods. I don't have a concrete plan yet, I'm getting a little chills, but it will pass, I have to be collected. I'll stop by the church afterwards to light a candle. A cell phone rings, a message from the Cop.

- Dominik, I'm waiting for you at 07:00 pm, you know the place.

I read the message and put the phone down. I knew that the fat man would sniff and press me, until he knew everything down to the smallest detail. It's five to twelve. To lubricate my rusty mental wheels. Act, Dominik, act, this is your last straw that you can hold on to and get out of the long-term fungus that threatens to swallow you with all that crazy head, I talked to myself in my mind. I'm going to church later. "Our Father who art in heaven", I automatically started saying the prayer and then switched to "Holy Virgin" and so on in a circle, until the clock struck 6:00, when my working hours ended.

I headed towards the church trying, as hard as I could, to strain myself to make up a story for the cop. I almost collided with Christine who was standing at the church gate, all crying and upset.

- For God's sake, Christine, what happened?
- No... some... someone... - she grunted and couldn't catch her breath.
- Take it easy, calm down. Come on, drink a glass of water and sit down, and you'll tell me.

I took her to the faucet at the gate, washed her and poured water for her to drink, and then I placed her on the bench so she could come to her senses. I waited a few minutes until she regained her composure and started talking on her own:

- Dominik, someone broke into the church shop.
- How? Did he hurt you?
- It's not. I was watering the flowers behind the church and when I was coming back, I saw a man running towards the gate, and a broken window of the shop. I didn't dare to do anything. I was afraid he would hurt me.

- Lord, in broad daylight, I was shocked: - What did that man look like, do you remember?

- Medium height, about one meter eighty, eighty kg, nothing impressive. The only thing was that he was extremely dark, like a gypsy...

I got goosebumps. The burglar matched Fatih's description. If this is true, he is a thief and a kleptomaniac, or there is something else that made him do this. I have to find out.

- I'll find him, I promise. And you pull yourself together a bit, maybe go home and take a nap. Did you tell the reverend?

- Yes, it will arrive in a minute.

- There he goes, I saw a priest with whom I did not like to talk. I had just enough time to avoid him and get out on the other side: - I'm going now, Christine, you won't be alone. I'm in a hurry, I have to buy medicine for the old Ma. I'll find that dark-skinned thief, don't worry.

- You don't need to, Dominik. We'll call the Cop. Thank you.

- Oh, you're welcome.

So, I went straight from the church to the meeting with the Cop. And I didn't light the candle, is that a bad omen?

XXXII

Fatih ran as if without a soul, dressed all in black, with a hood on his head. His shoes were dirty with mud, and his legs up to the knees were splattered with mud in confused shapes. He went under the bridge near the church to change into another sweatshirt he had in his backpack.

They must not recognize me, he thought as he looked back to make sure someone wasn't following him. He took the hood off his head and took out money from his pockets, which he folded with trembling fingers and wrapped with a rubber band, and then stuffed into the inner pocket of his rucksack. Then he took off his sweatshirt, crumpled it up and put it in a bag, which he then threw into the bushes. In that he went down to the river, washed his hands and face, cleaned his shoes and pants, then went back up, took out a spare blue sweatshirt and when he put it on, he looked back once more to make sure he was alone. Then he went out into the street as if nothing had happened.

He took out his cell phone and sent a message to Dominik: Wait for me in front of the building at exactly eight in the morning. I'm coming to pick you up in a van. Then he headed to the slot club for a game of poker. He waited there for the morning.

This is the last time, really the last time, I swear, he thought to himself, as he twirled the tips in his empty pockets with his dark circles drawn to the card table, where his Michael Corso watch still stood and his word that he would repay the debt in seven days at the latest or it is written in black.

XXXIII

Peter stood in front of the mirror, smoothed the little hair on the side of his balding head with both hands, raised his left eyebrow in satisfaction, and grinned at his reflection as he rubbed his palms together and thought of the rich catch to come and the title of senior inspector that he would proudly carry. How he will laugh in the face of that little conceited Denis, that kid will never be better than him.

Then he turned to the side and pulled in and pressed his stomach as far inside as possible with his right hand, so that he wouldn't appear to be as decently built as possible, and saliva was dripping from his mouth at the thought of the high school girls who would breathe after him when he got the rank.

It was 6:45. Time to go to the meeting to hear another rant from Dominik. He heard something, and it's not out of place to strut around the station until the big fish comes from Bosnia. He put on a short black coat that his mother had bought him back in high school and now it looked like it wasn't his. Compressed in the shoulders, and so narrow that he could not even fasten it, it stood on him like some ragged rag, under which the stomach was screaming, and behind was the rear. Nevertheless, despite such a tragicomic image, he was satisfied with himself, in the mirror he already saw an act and not a person.

XXXIV

I arrived at the garage shelters at 6:57. Even as I was approaching my destination, I saw the Cop happily taking long strides with those clumsy crooked fat legs, his arms flailing as if he was about to take off at any moment. He accepted himself well, I thought, what is your complex and vanity? If he continues like this, he will still have a line to polish. It would take the stars to raise me as a private guru, albeit on a temporary basis. When I plunge the knife of reality into his back, he is sobered to put an end to his playful marching and clapping of hands for all time and surrender forever to his usual sluggishness and grumpiness. I felt a little sorry for him, even though the garbage was unseen, but what's the matter, I'm on my way and better tomorrow, I've been the Cop's puppet enough. He will suffer, be played, but that's not my concern, he deserved it...

I put out my cigarette and went to my side of the garage stairs to wait for him there, so we wouldn't look suspicious together. It was already common practice and I could get to that place blindfolded.

Before approaching his place, the Cop looked around slightly to make sure that no one was watching him. After making sure that the situation was under control, he continued there. He lit a cigarette, transferred it to his left hand and wiped the sweat from his forehead with his right, and then he put on that grim, stern expression on his face, and put the cigarette in the left corner of his mouth, then he passed it between the middle finger and the index finger of his right hand, and as he exhaled the smoke, asked me a well-known question:

- What are you coming with, kid?

- Someone robbed the church store. - I said.

- And you don't know who it is? - he squinted with both eyes, with that questioning smile "I can see through everything, you won't escape me".

- No… not yet… but I'll find out… I think now…

- We should be dealing with something bigger, right?

- Well, yes. - I confirmed.

- Listen, kid, if you don't come back tomorrow with reliable and favourable information for our shop, watch out. And don't think you don't need to do anything until it's done as its your ass on the line. Clear?

- Clear... like day... I'll find out about the church... I'm meeting with the Bosnian in the morning. I made up a story that I had a good buyer for that weapon. He takes me to show me the goods in Bosnia. You have to be wise now...

- Little - he looked at me sternly as if he was going to slap me at any moment: - You should be the wise one, it's your head. You understand? If you had drawn me with the information here the day after tomorrow morning at 10:00 am or you would find out what solitary confinement looks like in the prison, long life to remember and look at it, every wall in that slobbery nose to absorb.

But he knows how to be obnoxious and sleazy. But it doesn't affect me anymore. I take all his outbursts calmly and calmly. Life has forced me to get into the smallest pore of the human psyche so much that, if I'm lucky and smart enough to get out of the clutches of this slob and run away somewhere, I believe I'll be able to refrain from providing psychotherapy services. Although, there will be no need for that, since, if everything goes according to plan, I will make a good living out of both him and the Bosnian and live like a kidney in fat. It has to be a "cash cart and trinket", so that "the bottom of my deep pocket is not visible".

- You understand? - the bald fat man repeated the question and took me out of my thoughts.
- Yes, yes… everything will be fine, Peter. Do not worry. The day after tomorrow I will come to you with detailed information, both for the church and for the Arabs. - I was extremely polite and contrite, only the halo of a saint was missing. I would also cheat on my own mother. How skilled a man is as an actor when he is forced to do so.

- Get the fuck out now. - the Cop said commandingly.

I obeyed the order without a word.

On the way to the apartment, I met old Tony. He yawned around the buildings and hunted where he could hear and transmit, the old buzzing - live video surveillance and radio transmission.

- Hello, Tony. - I answered politely.

- Well, kid, did you hear? - he immediately became eager to gossip and it was as if the whole world already knew what he wanted to talk about.

- What? - I passed a little so that I wouldn't shout, so that the whole neighbourhood wouldn't listen to us.

- Come here. - he invited me even closer to him so that he could whisper in my ear what he knew, as if it were a special secret, and he had already stopped who knows how many people before me:

- Did you hear that the church was robbed?

I love this old man who always seems to find himself when I'm pressed to the bone to give me exactly what I need.

- I heard it on the way, but I don't know what happened. You know something? - I asked completely disinterestedly, as if I didn't believe that the old man could know anything about it, and as if even if he knew, it didn't mean anything special to me.

- It is said that there was a black man, extremely black, wearing a hood... and I think... oh, no, it can't be...
- What do you think, Tony?
- I hope I'm wrong, but it's all suspicious to me... I think it's one of those new immigrants, one of those Arabs...
- Well, it can't be. - I feigned disbelief.
- I don't know, kid, I've seen you walking around with that black one. Take care.
- I'll take care, Tony. Thank you. - I left pretending to be in a hurry.

I have to be careful when I meet Fatih from now on. It will be better if we limit ourselves to the garage shelter. And is it possible that he robbed the church shop? I just can't believe it. They have so much money. "Come on, maybe that Arab half-brother is pulling him a bit, so he doesn't get to hunt as much as his appetites, so he wants to sell that marijuana, but if he goes so far as to rob a church

store... there must be some other story that I don't know
…

XXXV

After a sleepless night in the casino, Fatih went to the garage shelter to help his half-brother unload the goods. He dragged himself like carrion, eyes sunken, grey, dark circles halfway up his cheeks, dark, dark as the darkest point in the dark tunnel of vice he had fallen into.
Adin, who normally didn't like his half-brother because he wasn't a pure Arab, got even tougher seeing Fatih like that.

- What do you look like, you bastard? - he growled:
- And where are you until now?

Fatih just bowed his head and remained silent. He knew he was guilty and had nothing to say. Adin annoyed him a lot, and since he had nothing left to lose, he would have gladly punched him in the stomach, then under that imaginary nose to the sky under the clouds. In order not to get completely out of control, he was only held back by the thought of the deal he started with Dominik. He will swallow half an hour's reasoning and heavy insults, he will remain silent for the sake of the elders whom he greatly appreciated and pitied for having created him like this, and even worse for the fact that they also accepted Adin in the whole story. He hated him.

- It is his fault that I started gambling and stealing. He, only him. He took my father's love, won my mother. He was entrusted with the job, he was given the power of attorney for everything, while I am a simple pawn, a hidden workforce... and that's how it's always been. He was always older and smarter, more capable... Why, why everything to him? - thought Fatih, as he silently unloaded the truck and fought the desire to beat Adin to death, as if that would solve everything in his life.

During that time, Adin sat quietly on the pallets and smoked, looking at Fatih from above, confident and aware that he was the boss and that the little Bosnian, completely immersed in the sin of gambling, could do nothing for him.

XXXVI

I almost didn't close my eyes. Today I will take the first step towards freedom. I glance at the digital clock on the dilapidated dark walnut wooden table across from my bed. It's only twelve minutes past six. I probably have an hour and a half until it's time to get ready. I stare at the ceiling out of habit, it's become my regular rhythm. It seems to me that even if all the dice in my life fell into place right now, if I were no longer dependent on the Cop, if I were free and without problems, I would certainly continue to be committed to my ceiling and staring for at least a few more months. This went along with waking up and became an obstacle to washing and brushing teeth.

I didn't hear the old one. He's not going to work today. He must still be sleeping. Maybe I could make her happy today with breakfast. The poor thing, she is completely lost because of me, and I, the blind man, did not give a penny, I selfishly followed only my own needs. And what else could I do? Wasn't it enough that I protected her from knowing what kind of shit I'm in?! And that old bastard, if he was with her, it would be easier for her, both for her and for me. Maybe I wouldn't have become who I am, maybe I would have been a better man.

Time passes as I question myself and my actions, the influence of the environment, study DNA, family heritage, social situations and political games. It's only four minutes until seven o'clock, and I haven't even washed yet. How do you make fritters?

And maybe she wanted to drink coffee first?... And if my fries burn... I'll just put even more pressure on her. She's fragile anyway. I'm going to fry some eggs and run to the bakery across the street for fresh bread… yes, that… that's how I'll do it. It's seven hours and eleven minutes. I haven't washed yet. And what should I wear? Where is my blue hoodie?

I get up and turn things over in the closet. Eventually I found the sweatshirt all the way down behind some T-shirts. He's crumpled.

It doesn't matter, it can be done that way. Or should I still drive him? Will I act more seriously that way? And maybe I'll give the impression of a mollusc, a mama's boy? For God's sake, Dominik, it's a sweatshirt, not a silk shirt! I scolded myself: you're not going to walk like you've been chewed by cows, are you?! Where is the iron? Ahem... well... a blue sweatshirt and these jeans... great... Well, now to wash... It's seven hours and twenty-nine minutes. I have to leave in fifteen minutes... I haven't washed myself... and maybe I should say a prayer, at least one inside me... first I should wash myself...

There is a knock on the front door. Who is it now?

- Mother?

- Are you up, son?

- Yes, I am. And where were you? - I went to tell her that I was going to prepare breakfast, but then I glanced at the analogue wall clock in the living room and saw that it was almost fifteen to eight, and she was ahead of me.
- I went to my uncle's place to clean up for him and we had breakfast together. I kneaded the scone quickly. Uncle brought some cream; he was in the village yesterday... I brought it to you too. Come on, get ready and come eat. There is cake afterwards.

It's already fifteen to eight. I'm still standing at the bathroom door. I'm getting nervous. I will be late.

- Oh, mother... I'm in a hurry... I'm in a big hurry...
- So where are you going, it's Saturday?
- And…

Have I washed yet? I don't remember... and the prayer? It's five minutes to eight.

I run out the front door, almost knocking the old one over and say nothing.

I didn't wash.

The mother remained standing with the bags in her hands in the hall. Now he probably already thinks that

I'm in favour of a mental hospital... and it's probably not far from the truth...

XXXVII

My stomach howled like a wolf at the moon. I haven't put anything in my mouth since noon yesterday. I completely forgot that I should be eating. Actually, I should have made that breakfast. I don't know where I lost track of so many minutes and hours. I left the old whiny girl again. I am constantly involuntarily causing her severe mental suffering. How did I even get into all this? I have the impression that the Cop is constantly squeezing me around the throat, at times I simply physically feel that I am suffocating, grunting and unable to get air. I had to cut this off: or I will suffocate in my own stupidity, in that crushing swamp of sin and abomination in which I have sunk so much that I can only draw in some air of hope through my nostrils; or I will find the strength and jump out of that mushroom, no matter what risk the overall situation may bear. And the decision must fall on this second option, it must if I want to live. It hurts me that I am satirising the old Ma with my behaviour and actions, but I can't pay attention to that if I want to succeed in my intention to make that ugly image that I have been hiding from her for years become a thing of the past. Above all, she would certainly prefer to see me nervous and lost for a while, and not see me for a while, then to become mentally ill or worse, dead. I am aware that the game I got involved in can send me on a journey of no return and that instead of breakfast, my mother can soon prepare a coffin for me, but I also know that freedom has no price and that it is the most valuable and essential thing that I want to achieve, a sign of life, real life. Surely, she would rather see me nervous and lost for a while, and not see me for a while, than to become mentally ill or worse dead. I am aware that the game I got involved in can send me on a journey of no return and that instead of breakfast, my mother can soon prepare a coffin for me, but I also know that freedom has no price and that it is the most valuable and essential thing that I want to achieve, a sign of life, real life. surely, she would rather see me nervous and lost for a while, and not see me for a while, than to become mentally ill or worse dead. I am aware that the game I got involved in can send me on a journey of no return and that instead of breakfast, my mother can soon prepare a coffin for me, but I also know that freedom has no price and that it is the most valuable and essential thing that I want to achieve, a sign of life, real life.

XXXVIII

After helping his half-brother unload the truck, Fatih remained sitting on the pallets in the garage shelter. He lit up a joint, he got nervous, he had to relax a little. He would have preferred to beat Adin to death and cut off all contact with him, but he couldn't because he was completely dependent on him due to gambling.

Although he almost despised him for not being a pure-blooded Arab, Adin, out of respect for his father, always rescued Fatih from gambling debts and saved him from threats and, by God, from attempts to physically deal with those he owed. In the last month, he also got quite fed up, so he often left Fatih to himself. He no longer had the will or strength to get him out of the unpleasant situations he was getting into more and more often, and now that the old man was in Bosnia, he could neither control him nor have an insight into whether he helped his younger half-brother every time. That's how Fatih started to steal, gave himself more and more to gambling, and Adin became less and less interested, and more and more distanced himself and pretended to be blind to Fatih's problems.

He wandered a little more in his thoughts. He forgot to look at his watch. Somewhere in his head was that he had to meet Dominik at eight to go to Bosnia, but it seemed to him that he still had a lot until then. He was staring somewhere in the distance, lost for anything real around him, even for himself and his body. Only when the joint burned to his fingers and stained him did he wince.

- Uuuu... For fuck sake... I'm screwed?! - he cursed himself.

Dominik had been waiting for him outside for forty-five minutes. It was as if someone had spilled kerosene in his stomach as he was hungry.

- It turns out that old Tony was right. That Bosnian is a criminal. He must have robbed the church a little earlier and sneaked somewhere or he must be hiding. Yes, I am a moron! Should he run away from me now that the light at the end of the tunnel was within my reach. - thought Dominik.

At that moment, he heard him piling something in the garage shelter and Fatih cursing.

- I still need to catch fire, so that I can fall to that stinking piece of shit from my half-bro. Well, I won't give him that pleasure. I'm going to Bosnia as I planned. - Fatih hummed out loud: - Holy shit, what time is it! - he shouted in a daze.

In that, he looked towards the exit door and saw Dominik standing there.

- Bro, for God's sake, what are you doing? - Dominik asked in amazement.

- What am I doing... Getting bored. I thought you had already left...

- So, what do you look like?! Look at yourself! - exclaimed Dominik, seeing him with sunken cheeks, his worn out, and puffy, dilated pupils, as if only his eyes were left on his face, which were almost completely covered by dark circles.

- Adin is to blame for everything! His mother...

- What's wrong? Do not swear! You didn't help him all night, did you?

- Oh, I did, dude. It doesn't matter a bit, Fatih lied. We just finished. And I told him that I had to drive to Bosnia...

Dominik knew that this one was lying to him. Who is still high after a full night of unloading trucks. By the way, he knew that only one truck always comes, and that everything can be unloaded in a couple of hours. Something else was at stake, and he would discover it, only slightly. He will pretend to be naive and swallow this concoction for his personal, higher goal. Now it was necessary to step towards Bosnia, towards the gates of freedom.

- Well, poor thing. Come on, I'll drive. You swear the goods are good, right?
- There is no doubt about that, you will see everything. - Fatih blushed a little.
- Then you don't have to worry. I guaranteed you an excellent dealer. We will profit, both you and me. And then if you want, we can go to Hawaii together. Here's the hand.
- Here is the hand, confirmed Fatih.

They shook hands and got into the van heading toward Bosnia, Dominik in the driver's seat, and Fatih in the passenger's seat.

XXXIX

While the wheels of the van in which Dominik and Fatih were rolling towards Bosnia, Peter was sniffing around, trying to find out something about the newly arrived Arabs in the city.

After thoroughly searching the database at the Cop station, he went to the field. Something smells bad there, but that something will bring him success and reputation, he felt it. He informed his boss that he would not be coming to the office that day:

- Hello, inspector, it's Peter.

- Say - the senior inspector said coldly and disinterestedly, because the dupe cop was already pretty sick of calling him names for every little thing.

- Inspector, I'm on the trail of a major crime. I won't come to the office today. I have to examine everything in detail.

The inspector seemed to breathe a sigh of relief and was happier that he would not see a bald fat sycophant than that some big criminal story would be exposed: - All right, Peter. Do what you have to do and don't call me until you have the correct information. I'm in a rush today.

- Don't worry about anything. This is a big story, but I won't disturb you until…

Tu-tu, tu-tu... an empty telephone line stretched out. The inspector ended the call without listening to the Cop completely, but accustomed to his incoherent everyday ramblings.

Peter's little hair on his bald head stood on end, and if he could, he would have burst out of anger. - He will see - he muttered to himself: - Petra is breaking up, nice, nice... and when Denis comes, coffee is made, then they separate and cuddle, only they don't lick each other's asses... I'll show you all! You will remember who Peter Horvat is!

Visibly annoyed, he went towards the garage shelters where he usually met Dominik and where the Arabs were unloading goods. He couldn't calm down, his heart started beating hard and he was gasping for air.

- I'm just about to have a heart attack. - he thought. He stopped by a shop in Dominik's neighbourhood and bought a bottle of water, then sat down on a nearby bench for a while to vomit. Just as he took his first sip, he saw an old man with a cane, quite weak but determined in his step towards him as if it was of crucial importance to his good day. It was old Tony, eager for new stories and gossip. Peter did not know him. It seemed to him that he might have seen him around the neighbourhood, but they didn't have any close encounters because he always avoided being seen by anyone when he was with Dominik. And now he shouldn't have allowed himself to sit on that bench, but he wasn't really feeling well. But he's on duty, isn't he? - he thought: - Now there is nothing to hide. You should behave normally.

- Hey, Inspector! - old Tony spoke to him from three meters away: - Are you okay?
- I'm fine, man. - replied Peter coldly and seriously, determined to cut off any conversation even before it started.

Of course, that wasn't enough for Tony, and he wouldn't have gotten away with it even in front of Peter's sharper performance. His urge to gossip was stronger than any verbal barrier of the interlocutor. He would make even a mute person talk to him. And without asking, he sat down on the bench next to the Cop and immediately started a conversation:

- I was worried when I saw how pale you were. And you must be chasing some criminals... Well, all kinds of things really happen here... And that scandal yesterday in the church... they even robe the church...

Peter remained silent the whole time, hoping that the old man would get up and leave. Out of respect for his age, he refrained from being rude and driving him away, and on the other hand, he secretly hoped that the old man would mention the newly arrived Arabs in some context and give him some indication of where to look.

- Did you find them? - continued Tony.

- Who did I find? - said Peter.

- Well, them - those thieves.

- But what thieves, man?! Who are you to question me and interfere with my duties?

- Excuse me, please. I'm not curious, I'm just asking because I'm afraid of those... more and more people are scaring us... People are not allowed to go out on the street freely anymore. And those blacks... newcomers... They scare me the most... They say there was a black one there... - Tony continued chirping like a curious boy.

- Which black one? Where? - here the lights came on for Peter.

- Well, those black...new...Arabs, what are they?!

- And where were they? - now the Cop was already interested in talking.

- Well, the church shop when they robbed... that little Christine who works there... she said that there was a black man...

That's what it means. - Peter assembled the dice for himself and wondered if the old man knew anything about arms smuggling. He was looking for words to indirectly question him. He did not have the developed ability to read the human psyche like Dominik. That's what he needed that little one for.

- Arabs steal around the corner, don't they? - asked Tony.

- I do not know. That's what I heard. They have some big vans and trucks; they opened a place downstairs with a betting shop and slot machines... It's a mafia guarantor.

- What waters are they in, you...how do you know that? - Peter asked cautiously.

- Well, I don't know, I tell you, but please pay attention to them. They are totally suspicious to me. Where do they get so much money from?

- Be calm, old man. - the Cop feigned professionalism: - the Zagreb police are always up to the task... Now excuse me, I have to go.

- You'll let me know if you find out. - Tony stared at him like a cat on bacon, gossip was his soul food.

The Cop just looked at him sideways and got up from the bench.

- No offence…I'm just concerned for my safety. - kept shouting Tony, while the Cop was walking away behind the buildings.

He hid there and waited for the old man to leave so that he could enter the garage shelter unhindered and snoop through the packages left by the Arabs.

XL

Fatih was so exhausted from not sleeping and stunned by the grass that he did not move from his place to the border with Bosnia. He wouldn't have even looked there, if Dominik hadn't been forced to wake him up because he didn't know where to go or where exactly Fatih's cousin's house was.

The rain poured down like a river, Dominik could hardly see where he was driving. In addition, he was hungry as hell and that made him nervous and made it impossible for him to control his movements.

- Why didn't we eat something before leaving? - he wondered: - Am I so crazy and lost that I can't gather my body and thoughts in one place all morning?... And he's sleeping... How can he look so peaceful after the state in which I found him a moment ago? Shall I stop somewhere to eat something?...

With that thought, he felt the left pocket of his sweatpants where he usually kept his wallet.

- Oh, fuck - he cursed out loud: - I forgot my wallet.

Fatih did not react at all to Dominik's shout. He slept as if he had been slaughtered, as the old people would say.

- And the documents? Where did I leave them? Let's put aside the fact that I'm hungry, and how am I going to cross the border?... Fuck, there aren't any... Oh, I'm very hungry...

His hands were shaking and he was no longer able to think normally. He opened the compartment in front of the passenger seat to see if there were any chips or anything else inside to put in his mouth, but there was nothing there but documents. He couldn't hold on any longer, not even a mile. He saw a supermarket on the right. He stopped the van. It was early and a lot of people went to do their morning shopping. He took advantage of the crowd to put some buns in a bag under his sweatshirt and a tube of mini salami - the popular burp. He put on an innocent expression and pretended to be looking for fresh meat, which was not normally available in that supermarket:

- Excuse me sir, they don't sell fresh meat here? - he asked the elderly man by the refrigerator with dairy products.
- No, there isn't. You have a butcher shop two streets down. - answered the man politely, not suspecting anything.
- Thank you.

He pretended to be naive again and left the store. He immediately got into the van. He barely lasted two hundred meters. He didn't even stand anywhere. He was holding that salami with one hand and opening it with his teeth, and then he was voraciously biting as if he were eating a banana. He did the same with buns. He was so hungry that, it seemed to him, he would have eaten ten times more, if only he had had it. After about fifteen minutes, when his brain finally sent him the information that he was full, he could finally think normally. The border with Bosnia was close. It was supposed to wake up Fatih somehow.

- And what will I do without a document? I have to think of something. I can't stop it now that I've come this far. I will cross the border at least through an underground tunnel, through the forest, flying or on all fours...

XLI

There, close to the border, Dominik stopped the van on the extension on the right side of the road.

- Fatih... hey, Fatih - first he quietly called the Bosnian, then a little louder: Fatih, hey, wake up. Then he put his right hand on his shoulder and shook him slightly, then with both hands on both shoulders. This one did not show any reaction, he was still fast asleep, occasionally snoring softly as if to signal that he was alive and to warn him not to be touched while he was sleeping. Dominik also tried to pull his eyelid between his thumb and forefinger and force him to open his eye, but he stubbornly squinted as if his eyelids were made of lead.

- This doesn't work at all - thought Dominik: - but I have to wake him up as best I know how. He has to drive... and how is he going to drive like this? Oh, we're about to perish.

At that moment, he saw a brandy bottle in the door next to the passenger seat. He didn't think much or calculate the outcomes and consequences. He grabbed that bottle and threw it all over Fatih's face.

- This will surely sober you up, you high-spirited cattle! - he said out loud.

Fatih started vomiting and blowing alcohol out of his nose and waving his arms uncontrollably as if he was going to swim.

- Holy shit, what is this? – like the coachman's speech woke him up and galloped from his insides: pppp... he was blowing... what the fuck are you doing man?

Dominik couldn't help laughing at first, but when he saw that he was swinging to hit him, he put on a serious expression:

- Calm down! Slowly. - said a voice like a guru or psychotherapist: - I'm sorry, I've been waking you up for more than half an hour, there was no way I could even remove an eyelash from you...

- So, you poured brandy on me? - Fatih hissed a shade less furious.

- I had no choice, bro. I have no documents, I forgot or lost them somewhere. You'll have to hide me somewhere and you'll have to drive.

- Fuck it - thundered Fatih: - so, what are you thinking about?! And what will we do if they find you? Where, sick, should I hide you, lucky you?

- Well, I do not know. Dominik shrugged his shoulders innocently.

Aware that this story might be more necessary for him than for Dominik, because his head is already at stake, he decided to stop the discussion and quickly engage his brain to place the "blind traveller" somewhere.

- Well done... Come on, man, see if there's a tent wing in the back, it was there.

Dominik quickly jumped up as if on military orders and pulled out the tent wing from behind.

- Here it is.

- Well, we'll do it this way: I'll wrap you in it and pull you under the seat, and you don't move, don't breathe and don't peek until I tell you it's safe. Clear?

- Like a day. - where he is now allowed to oppose, the Bosnian would grind him down.

They placed Dominik under the back seat, and then Fatih lined up the boxes with the goods that he would show at the border so that nothing would be suspicious. He didn't have money to bribe the customs officer, so he took out the original Armani Code perfume from one of the boxes to put in with his documents.

XLII

- Your documents, please. - said the customs official when Fatih opened the window.
- There you go, he held out his passport with a box of perfume underneath.
- And what is this? - asked the already visibly pleased customs officer, peering under the passport to see which perfume it was.
- It's from the heart. - Fatih smiled slightly.
- Have you been drinking? Do you smell like alcohol?
- Ohh, no... Uncle spilled his brandy yesterday when he was going to the village - Fatih managed.
- Well, that's not going to happen, is it? I know how it is. And you are in business, do you sell perfumes?

- Well, yes... - Fatih was sweating.

- My wife likes that Black Opium a lot, we can't find it anywhere...

- Well, what don't you say?! I have exactly that one.

He turned the whole bag over until he found the perfume he was looking for.

- Here it is.

- And you really tried. Of course, it's from the heart?

- Of course, of course, the house honours your wonderful lady.

- Well, you shouldn't have. Thank you. - but what is it, the customs officer thought as he adjusted the artificial smile: - Here are your documents. Have a nice trip!

That's how they got through with the Croats, now it was the turn of the Bosnian border guard who was not so sweet and venal. He asked Fatih to throw all the things out of the van, checked the documents, wandered around, ransacked. Fortunately, he didn't look under the seat. Dominik was so scared that he literally stopped breathing. When the Bosnian finally let them go, it seemed to him that he would not be able to breathe for days.

- Uuuu... we passed... - screamed Fatih, as if he had been saved alive from the gallows: - Get out, man, the coast is clear.

Dominik just panted and remained silent.

- Breathe, breathe, for God sake... It can't be like this next time. Settle the border with your guys, you heard.

Dominik just nodded his head, still unable to catch his breath.

XLIII

"Radio Free Europe: Special units of the criminal police detained a 39-year-old citizen of Bosnia on suspicion of being connected to the terrorist attacks in Paris..." - was the first thing that was heard when Fatih turned on the radio in the van.

- Well, we are having a good time in this Bosnia of yours! We just found the right time to come and make deals. I hope that's not your cousin.
- Be silent, be grateful. You should thank me for pulling your head alive over a border.
- It's not you, but your half-bro, if you didn't have his perfumes, I would have crossed the border in no

time - I already started joking because I was relieved, I was scared like never before. Yes, I'm a snitch, but in a nutshell, I've never even faced real danger.

- That's why you will ensure the crossing next time.

- Nope, you will?!

- God, it's going to be serious, there's no room for kidding.

In the story and the jokes, time passed to Fatih's cousin Sakib's house in the city of Foča.

It was a two-story house, with a two-meter-high wrought-iron gate and the same height of concrete walls enclosing a huge yard. At the gate, of course, we were met by a mutt, no less than a Rottweiler, who growled and climbed up the bars of the gate with drool running down his muzzle as if he was being consumed by hunger and couldn't wait to tear us apart.

If this one doesn't dissect us like frogs, neither the Cop nor the terrorists will - I thought. I stood as if buried and could not even say the letters.

- Come on, what have you got yourself into? He won't do anything. - said Fatih's cousin who suddenly appeared at the gate: - Come, Trampy.

Listen to me, Trampy. Well, that beast, and there's Trampy. Cuddles would probably be too, if she were female. - I still didn't move.

- Come on, come on in! Maybe you won't have a red carpet. - said Sakib while the dog caressed his body and licked his hand, or rather washed it, because his tongue covered a surface equal to a standard shower and produced saliva under a full stream.

The dog didn't even move when we entered, but my heart was still in my heels. When we got to the front door, Sakib came after us. First, he typed in a sixteen-digit code, and then unlocked two locks with more keys. Everything inside was bursting with expensiveness and luxury. He ushered us into the living room and ordered us to sit on the leather corner sofa. He adjusted himself in the armchair and invited the guy to serve us drinks.

- Whiskey, guys, okay? I have a superb Aberlour.

That name didn't mean anything to me, it could have said whiskey, but it already sounded elite to me. The only alcohol I've tried in my life was my uncle's plum wine and wine for weddings, beer not to be counted as alcohol, not even the Russians until recently. The old Ma was a bit afraid of alcohol because of the old man, because he knew that he was getting drunk and massaged her in such a state when I was little. I guess that stuck in my memory, so I avoided getting drunk, and because of such an upbringing and the economic crisis, I didn't have the opportunity to explore the tastes of alcoholic beverages.

The young man poured us whiskey and left without saying a word.

- Let me see what you offer me. - Sakib spoke to us while, with an icy face, shooting us with a sharp look, reclining in an armchair, in a black department that seemed to command that the boss is the one who wears it, as strong as the devil himself and those who are with him should be careful enter into any contracts.

XLIV

I swallowed a huge dumpling before I could speak. I observed Sakib's black ring with a huge stone on the ring finger of his right hand. It seemed to me that if I said anything that would partially displease him, he would smash me in the head with that stone so that I would remain dead on the spot.

Fatih seemed calm and self-confident, probably because he knew his cousin from earlier and knew which way he could aim.

I sat as if buried, I wasn't allowed to lift a finger, not even to twist the thread sticking out of my sweatpants to calm my nerves.

Fatih spoke first:

- Sakib, I told you about Dominik. He has a good dealer there in Croatia...

- Are you? That's all I've heard. - Sakib cut him off: - Now I want to see what he has to say, provided he knows how to speak, or has the cat eaten his tongue, huh? - he said and shot me that murderous icy look.

I reached for the whiskey and drained it to the bottom. I have to look like I know what I'm doing and that I'm some big brain in the world of crime in Croatia, otherwise I'll lose my head. Whether it was from the alcohol or from the simmering fear that I would completely fail if this didn't work out, I suddenly got some superhuman strength and confidence in myself, and I finally spoke as loudly and confidently as if I had always been preparing for this moment.

- My friend wants to be discreet. You will do all the work through me. So, I take goods and money from both.

- I just hope this isn't another one of your tricks to get out of gambling debts, Fatih. - said Sakib, a bit aggravated, which showed that this is not the first time that Fatih has put him in such situations: - If you need money, better tell me, you will do it for me. Don't drag me.

I did not allow Fatih to answer. I immediately cut it off:

- What do you think, who are you dealing with? I represent a serious clientele in Croatia. The biggest players cooperate through me, do you understand?! You are small fish to them. They are not crazy enough to reveal their identity to you, give you their address and phone number.

- Wow, this little one of yours is dangerous, Fatih.

I just glared at him.

- I'm Dominik for you.

- Okay, well, let's not blame each other. You must understand that I am suspicious. This little guy has brought me many problems in my life. I have to be careful. But this is how you and I will come

to an agreement so that no one would be harmed
or have to worry about being tricked.

- I set the conditions here. - I drummed as if I had
always done this job and had it in the palm of my
hand.

- Good, boy! Will you listen to me? I respect you,
but I can't give you goods for nothing.

- No one here talked about giving away. My man
pays fairly. I want to see the goods first.

- Let's go see now, but just so you know. I only
accept clean diamonds, and 20% in advance.

- There will be no problem - I remained calm and
sure of what I was saying: - You just make sure
that the goods are first class.

XLV

Sakib was not a man to waste time. He was engaged in
the work he was engaged in, but his word, when it was
yes, was sacred, it was also seen in his eyes - they were
as cold as a law that prescribes reward and punishment
regardless of gender, age, social or religious status. A
silent look was enough for me to know that he would not
try to deceive me, which I could not claim for Fatih, even

though I had known him for a long time and had already talked openly with him about some important and intimate topics for him. It always seemed to me that Fatih was hiding something from me. And that robbery that happened in the church, although I didn't even think about asking him, and I refused to ask myself if he was involved in it, some worm of doubt was constantly biting my subconscious in small bites.

- Here, gentlemen, follow me. - said Sakib, getting up from the armchair and heading towards the exit. In front of him and behind him walked a young man, also dressed in a black suit, like him, and with a pistol at his waist.

Sakib left nothing to chance, and it was clear that he was very suspicious of Fatih.

We went down to the yard and he motioned for us to sit in the back of his BMW 5 series with tinted windows. One of the guys who was in charge of driving us sat in front, and Sakib drove off with the other guy in a black jaguar. We didn't drive for long. The plantation was on a hill in a clearing, surrounded by beech and pine forest on all sides. The road was very narrow, unpaved and you could see that for years very few people had passed by on foot, let alone by car. Sakib's drivers seemed to have lost their minds, so they drove over the potholes as if they were sailing through the air. I was a little sick, but I endured everything for the sake of freedom, which I could already smell now.

Our driver got out first and opened the door for us, and only after us was Sakib with the guy who was driving him and guarding his back. Both boys stood by him again. I felt like an important and dangerous animal when a man needed protection to walk with me through an uninhabited area. Marijuana grew green and sprouted in the spring sun while the wind gently blew it. It seemed to me that everything was in rhythm: "green, I love you" that kept going through my head.

- Well, what say you, gentlemen? - Sakib proudly addressed us.

At that question, the record on the gramophone in my head turned to the other side, and when the needle went down to the beginning, the song blared out at its maximum: "The rain is falling, the grass is growing, the mountain is green..."

- Close your mouth, flies will fly into you. - Sakib joked, seeing how Fatih and I silently watched the plantation, mesmerized.

- What a fucking expanse! - I finally spilled the words.

- Well, what do you say - we made a deal? Twenty percent in diamonds in advance when you come to pick up the goods, and the rest when the goods reach the customer, and as a deadline I give you a month for that?

- At my word?! - I asked, already ready to say yes to everything he suggested, because I certainly had no plans to honour even part of the deal, let alone to cooperate longer. That's why it was more convenient for me to have everything at my word, if I was arrested somewhere, so that I would have more grounds to pretend to be stupid and get out of the dead end more easily.

- Do you doubt my word? - Sakib asked rhetorically.

- I see that you are a man of your word, there is no room for doubt.

- Then here's the hand. - said Sakib and I accepted and we shook hands warmly.

- So, I'm expecting you soon when you've sorted out the payment details to be sure. - he concluded: - And now you will forgive me. I have some work to do. The Emir will take you to the Croatian border so that you don't suffer, then cross the Polish road near the city of Bihać into Croatia. A taxi will be waiting for you there. Everything is paid for, don't worry.

- It was immediately clear to me that this Sakib is also smuggling illegal migrants.

He didn't wait for us to say anything. He got into his car, closed the door, and his driver drove him down a different route towards the city.

XLVI

Emir gestured for us to get into the car. We didn't say a word, and we entered as if under orders. We knew that any opposition or philosophizing could provoke Sakib's anger through the Emir, and that was not in the interest of Fatih or me. We had to trust him. There was no going back, and there was only one way forward. What is the light or the abyss at the end, we could only ask ourselves. We had to walk because there was no deeper mud than the one, we were both in.

Belief in a good outcome in itself, and each of us had to think so, Machiavellian observing a world in which no one else matters, that was the only possible choice, a struggle for bare life.

As I suspected, Sakib kept his word. Emir transported us across the border. Another taxi driver actually met us there and safely transported us to Zagreb. Neither one nor the other uttered any letters, nor addressed us with any gesture, neither of us dared to start a conversation either with them or between ourselves. We knew we should get into that taxi when we saw it, we knew we shouldn't say goodbye or thank you. All these 'commands' were read in Sakib's look when he left.

After getting out of the taxi at the entrance to Zagreb, we had to walk to our apartments. It was as if the command was still in effect and we didn't say a word. We were tired from the trip, I was sleepless, Fatih was probably hungry, each of us was sorting through our thoughts in our heads. At the building, we said goodbye by raising our hands and silently made an agreement that we would talk to each other later.

XLVII

Peter was already tapping away in his armchair in front of the computer at work. It was late afternoon. He tried several times to reach Dominik, but his phone was switched off. He knew that it would be like that until he returned, so that the Bosnian wouldn't suspect something, but shouldn't it have been until now that they returned? - he wondered. He got up and walked four laps around the desk. He sat down in the armchair again, tried to work, but it didn't work at all. He walked another four laps and then grabbed his coat from the hanger to get dressed and go outside. Just at that moment, he received an SMS that Dominik was available again.

He immediately called him.

Dominik wasn't really in the mood to talk to the Cop, he wasn't in the mood to talk to anyone, but he had to call.

- Hello... - he barely said anything, either because of tiredness or because of so much silence, as if he had lost or forgotten the words, they are easily used.

- Where are you so far? - thundered Peter from the other end of the line.

- Ahhh... mmm... - Dominik struggled until he finally caught the form of a word with meaning: - Mmm... Well, I've arrived now.

- What's wrong with you? Have you lost the power of speech? Talk - what did you discover?

- I discovered everything and everything is settled. I just don't think it's for a phone conversation.
- Then as soon as you have drawn yourself, you know where.

He hoped she wouldn't say that. He was dead tired and only fantasized about bed. However, he did not dare to object. The Cop knew this, and had already hung up without waiting for Dominik to give him an affirmative answer, it was understood that he would come.

XLVIII

I was hoping to at least get some rest. Why did I even turn on the damn cell phone? Why didn't I play dead until tonight? Look, Peter shit-eater, if he could he would drink my blood to the last drop, he sent me twelve messages, so that my inbox explodes... But I'm counting on sweat... phew... phew... maybe that will prevent him from staying with me longer than necessary.

I headed towards the garage shelter and waited for the Cop by the stairs where we always were. He arrived as quickly as if a helicopter had brought him. Well, it's nice when they rush into your arms, if only for the sake of taking advantage of you, I thought ironically: - I'm really loved and appreciated. He didn't even call me good morning, as usual. It was part of his culture and gentle nature. He immediately launched into a topic of importance to his butt:

- And kid, what do you say? Where the Arabs hide their weapons.

There was no time to hesitate, I had to act quickly, even though I hadn't planned any story in advance. I hoped he wouldn't start strangling me as soon as I arrived. Now, what's here is: Turn on, Dominik, all the cerebral gyro and activate all the psychological abilities:

- I discovered a lot. And I have a plan, but we have to keep everything a secret...

- Don't worry. Get to the point. - he was an impatient policeman.

- Here, here... take it easy... So, weapons are being smuggled from Syria. He goes by ship from the port to Greece, and then via Serbia to Bosnia, and from there that Bosnian and these Arabs here transport him to Zagreb. They bring smaller quantities, together with textiles so that it is not suspicious.

- And what do they intend with those weapons? Terrorist attack.

- Not here. But they sell weapons across the border to terrorists in Europe.

- What are you talking about?

- Don't worry, I've figured out how to arrest them and stop them once and for all.

- You mean the Cop or me?

- Yes, I mean you… er… I'm just a secondary link…

- That's right... and what did you do? Where do they agree to intercept them?

- Like this… I talked to that chief. I introduced myself as an agent for arms smuggling to terrorists in Europe and we arranged for them to send me the boxes through the Arabs in Banja Luka next Friday... but they want to be paid in diamonds, 20% in advance or they won't give the goods. Can you fix it?

All for glory, Peter thought to himself:

- I'll figure it out. Just don't let it be a scam, because I will find you and take your head off.

- What comes to your mind? When have I let you down so far?... Rather, we need to settle the border. Can you fix that too?

- Everything will be taken care of. You finish your part, I'll finish mine. I'll talk to you when everything is ready... Now get out of here. You're stinking like garbage men.

When he felt that I smelled, he could tell what time it was, I thought.

- We're on the line, I said and headed for my apartment.

He stayed for a while until I stepped back, so they wouldn't see us together.

XLIX

Fatih lazily strolled to his apartment. He smelled like a medieval stableman and was as hungry as an Ethiopian, but the amount of fatigue he carried on his back and in his head outweighed the unbearable stench of sweat and the hole in his gut. He didn't even take off his shoes. He immediately fell into bed and snored, if only he could sleep the sleep of the righteous...

L

After breaking up with Dominik, Peter also went to his apartment. It was too late, and he hadn't slept the night before either, as if he had travelled with Fatih and Dominik. An unbearable restlessness flared in him. It was necessary to sort out everything and finally get hold of the title of senior inspector. No matter how restless he was, he would have gone to work immediately, but the dismissal of his superior was complete and he was not allowed to call him even in his madness. He will take painkillers; it will calm him down and put him to sleep. Tomorrow he will move from thoughts to actions.

LI

Dominik could finally take a half-breath. For now, everything is going according to plan. If it were a normal situation, he would be dragging himself like a carrion right now. He almost bounced in his step like this. Ways are opening up for him. He will be free as a bird on a branch. He entered the apartment with a cheerful whistle. He took off his dirty clothes and put them in the washing machine. He bathed, shaved, and cut his nails.

- Now they can bury me - he thought: - This is a turning point: - either I will fly to the sky under the clouds for my freedom or I will sink to the black earth in eternal Hades.

He put on his underwear, changed the sheets and fell asleep in the blink of an eye, after a long time, with a smile on his face.

LII

- Get up, bums! - shouted Adin, shaking Fatih: - Get up, you carrion, you smell like a pig.

Fatih was still sleeping with his mouth wide open and snoring so loudly that the whole room was roaring. Seeing that he was not going to wake him up easily like this, Adin took a glass of water and splashed it in his face. At that, Fatih jerked and jumped off the bed into a sitting position, then started waving his hands in front of him.

- What the hell is this, for fuck sake?! - he cursed.
- Get up, stinky stinker! - thundered Adin: - I'm off to shower, then to work. Shame on you!
- Fuck, I'm hungry... - Fatih was spinning, as if he didn't hear what he was saying. It started a little bit perfect that his ear hurts for everything. Soon, Adin, Bosnia, and Croatia will be a thing of the past when he tricks Sakib and Dominik and runs away to Hawaii with diamonds. Until then, he'll

have to feign fear of his hated half-brother a little longer.

- Take a shower, I said! - repeated Adin, all enraged.

- Here, here... now. Don't be angry, it's not good for beauty. - Fatih challenged him, going towards the bathroom.

- You will see very soon you piece of shit...! - Adin waved his hand at him, but he had already run into the bathroom and slammed the door in his face.

LIII

Peter woke up late. It was past eleven. The painkiller stunned him. It seemed to him that he was sleeping among the clouds. Everything was so soft and tucked away, not even a fly was heard. He had the day off, but he couldn't wait until the next day to talk to the senior inspector. He wanted to show himself as someone who works outside of working hours. He put the kettle with water on the stove and, still unwashed (an activity he often knew how to skip - washing was neither important nor a mandatory daily routine for him), he reached for his cell phone to call his superior and tell him what he found out. Soon he will be rewarded, everyone will have to bow down to him and appreciate him, he will be Peter the shark, fearless, the strongest senior inspector of Zagreb. He coughed to adjust his voice before the connection was made:

- Good afternoon, inspector. - he answered politely.

- Good day, Peter. What good? Don't you have a day off today?

- It is true, Inspector, but I have made an important discovery. This is a big deal and it can't wait.

- What happened so important? There won't be another war, surely.

- Well, not far from it.

- What are you talking about? - now the inspector really focused on what Peter was telling him.

- Inspector, weapons for terrorists in Europe are being smuggled through our country. It's true.

- Come to the station now. We can't talk about this over the phone. I'm taken aback.

- Don't worry, I'll be there in a few minutes. Everything will be solved, I have a plan, people, everything. - Peter soothed him, all turned into honey and milk, he was a real sycophant, he would smear him on bread as much as he knew how to pamper himself when something important to his ass.

-   Come on, I'm waiting for you. - said his superior and they hung up.

LIV

Dominik woke up a little before nine, with a smile, as he had fallen asleep. He breathed in the smell of clean sheets and freshly washed hair that smelled of birch shampoo. He turned on the radio. This time he chose a music station, he won't be listening to the news today. The old one was in procurement. He aired the house, vacuumed and put the dirty laundry in the washing machine, took a shower, scrubbed the bathtub and ironed his white shirt and beige pants. He wanted to look nice. Now he is going out into the world for his freedom. He will be a new man.

He made coffee and made fries for himself and his mother. There was no need for him to think about whether he would succeed. Today, everything went well for him.

At that moment, the mother appeared at the door. A blissful smile spread across her face.

- God, Dominik - she said and cried with happiness. Dominik approached her, hugged her, then put his hands on her shoulders and looked into her eyes:

- Why are you crying, mother? Did I do something wrong?

- Oh, how beautiful you are... how... - she couldn't hold back her tears of joy. She felt for a long time that her son was depressed, that something was wrong with him. She was so happy to see him happy and smiling again.

- Come on, come. Come eat.

- Oh, and you also prepared breakfast... my son, my darling...

- Mother, please don't cry anymore. All is well.

- I know, I know, honey. - she wiped her tears, then fell silent for a few moments. She took a sip of coffee, smelled the fried food as if she was inhaling joy on credit with that smell, then looked at Dominik again: - You fell in love, didn't you?

- I did, mother. - we told her what she wanted to hear. He wanted to see her happy. They may never see each other again. When he leaves, if he survives, he must not return to Croatia.

- Well, who is she, son, will you tell me?

- You don't know her, mother. We have known each other for some time. She is from Germany.

- Tonight, I have to go on a trip with my colleagues from my new job, I have to help them with the goods, I have to express myself at my new job and work extra. I'll be back soon

- Tonight? So out of the blue? Why didn't you tell me anything earlier?

- I didn't know either. They called me last night.

- The mother was silent. She will miss him. She will be lonely to travel often, but his happiness was above all else for her. Dominik knew and felt it.

He took the bag, packed some clothes and kissed the old Ma on the forehead: - I have to go. I will call you. - he said and left the apartment.

- Goodbye, son, my Ma barely said, unable to get up from the chair, at the same time devastated by the pain that her only son would be far away and immensely happy that his life had finally started.

LV

Peter told the senior inspector more or less everything that Dominik had told him, leaving out the part about the diamonds because he was convinced that his superiors would not support the idea of getting involved from that side to solve the case. But he knew that there were diamonds in the station that were being kept as evidence, and he thought of borrowing them to trick the Arabs into handing over their weapons to Dominik, and when he put them behind bars, he would return the diamonds and no one would notice.

His cell phone rang in his pocket, which he used specially to communicate with Dominik. He forwarded him the photos that Sakib had sent him from his basement. Those were gun cases in which he kept marijuana, but of course the Cop didn't know that.

LVI

Everything was adjusted as if I had suddenly become the screenwriter of my life and all the other figures were moving according to my preconceived idea. Just when I was thinking about where to find some boxes of weapons to send to the Cop as evidence, Sakib took pictures of the two tons of weed he kept in the basement, along with the same boxes in which he kept most of the goods. Oh, is this paradise or did I dream?! I immediately forwarded the photos to fat Peter via mobile phone:

- This is potentially the biggest deal ever. Just solve the Croatian border so that they don't ask for my passport so that we don't complicate things further. I'm going there on Friday with a character from the Arab group. Have you secured payment?

- Give me some time. I'll get back to you during the day. Everything will be solved. I'm currently in a meeting with the inspector. - answered the Cop.

- I think it's only fair that you give me 10% commission and leave me alone after this. - I blackmailed him because I felt I could.

- OK, agreed. You have my word. - perhaps for the first time, he granted my requests, without objection or threat. "Everything for the glory of our Peter the Pig, for progress in rank for our Zagreb's Pig" - the verses kept running in my head.

Not long after, the cell phone rang. He must be calling me again to meet to tell me how he got on with the inspector, I thought, but I was wrong. The message was from Fatih. He called with new conditions. Sakib felt that he had both of them in his fist, so now he played with us like chess pieces, and we followed his orders like obedient pawns because he was the commander who decided whether to checkmate us or lead us to victory.

- Now that you have seen the goods, you have seen that we can load and that I have an alibi. As Sakib told you, the payment is in diamonds, but he is also asking for a 20% advance, and when loading, we send him a picture of the other diamonds as a guarantee. Can you fix it?

I'm quite afraid of how everything will turn out, because this is a big bite, but I got caught in the circle, I can't get out of the circle, so I play and weave my legs, and who will be the ringleader at the end and where this will take us, will only be revealed.

- Everything will be solved. - I answer briefly, as if I'm painfully confident and already have all the information.

LVII

- I leave the case to you and expect you to solve it, alone this time. I won't send you help. This is your chance to prove yourself. - said the senior inspector to Peter: - If everything you are telling me is true and if you put that Arab group behind bars, I will personally advocate that you be given a higher rank.
- Thank you, thank you, thank you - repeated the Cop like a broken record. He got so into the role that he almost knelt down and started bowing to the senior inspector and kissing his feet.
- It's good, it's good! - he raised his voice a little to alert him: - I have work to do now, and so do you, and a lot of it. Come on, get up!
- You won't regret trusting me, you'll see! - said Peter and left the office.

He came to his senses in an instant, for a bit of glory he would immediately turn on all the windings of his hollow head, but that was enough for the Cop, they were protected by laws and some higher power, I guess even God has more mercy on stupidity, it is not a threat to humanity. He went to the office where the evidence was kept and took a picture of the diamonds and forwarded the photo to Dominik via cell phone.

- Here. This is evidence. When are you going there? To call to resolve the border. We just have to react quickly so that the Cop doesn't find out that evidence is missing.

Dominik immediately spoke up:

- Friday night. Solve everything and wait for us at our border on the way back. We are on the line.
- Okay. - answered the Cop shortly.

Then he called a guy at the border who handled everything he needed for him, the same for a small fee or under blackmail like Dominik.

- Listen, kid, you're on duty Friday night. Do you understand? Set up a shift.
- What figure?
- Don't be rude. You immediately ask for the number. Do the work first. You will be richly rewarded, more than ever before.
- Really?!
- Not babbling! A van, Bosnian plates, an Arab company, one of my men and one of the Arab group will pass. See that they pass, don't ask for their passports. Clear?

- Like a day.
- Well, I'm glad to hear that. Hi. - the Cop ended the call and started rubbing his palms with satisfaction.

LVIII

On the same day, I met the Cop at the old place.

- We won't hold back, just so I can take over the advance payment for the weapons. The advance is 230,000 euros. - I previously wrote to him in an SMS message.

Now I was setting the conditions. In fact, I was supposed to take over 300 kg of weed with Fatih, the price of which was much lower, but I pumped it myself, because as Hitler said: The bigger the lie, the easier people will smoke it. Weapons and bombs are a dangerous business and it costs money, and the Cop knows that and would be suspicious if the number is lower when it comes to such things.

He brought the diamonds in a black drawstring bag. I asked him to open the bag so I could see them live. I was overshadowed by their light. They smelled of freedom.

- Did you fix the border? - I asked.

- Everything is under control. - He said.
- Let them not take my passport so we don't complicate things. - I emphasized once more.
- Just do your thing. The border has been resolved. I'm waiting for you on our side. And don't let me dream of you! - underlined the fat one to show me who is the boss.

Just wave, I thought to myself, I'll hold on a little longer, and then I'll leave for my freedom.

LIX

Fatih was waiting for me in the company's van in front of the building exactly at 20:13. We were supposed to do everything there during the night, rest, and then leave in the evening and return to Zagreb before morning.
Not long after we left the city, the Cop confirmed to me that the border was clear. Fatih's men settled the Bosnian border. The Bosnians needed a little more time, but they nicely hid the goods so that they could not be seen among the textiles and similar things that Fatih had to drive to the Arabs for the company.
I handed Sakib the agreed amount. He is satisfied.

- I see you are breathing fairly. - he says: - I expect
  continued cooperation.
- And the goods are first class, my associate is
  satisfied. I am sure that we will cooperate for a
  long time.

We shake hands, Fatih also shakes hands with him, and we get into the van, ready for the journey back. From the diamonds I have left, and there is quite a bit left over because I inflated the cop's price beyond belief, I give Fatih a couple of stones.

- Just that? - he asks me and looks disappointed.
- What else are you going to do? Do you know how
  much that's worth? - I calmly answer. I see that he
  is not quite right, so I say: - He gave me that
  much, there will be more when we sell the goods.

I see that he is looking at me strangely, I feel some restlessness, but I try to ignore him. You with your premonitions, for God's sake Dominik, come to your senses. Endure to the limit. Then the Bosnian belongs to the Cop, and freedom is yours. - I convinced myself. However, the fear of uncertainty washes over me. Will the cop do his job or will we hang? Fatih drives, so I can focus on my thoughts, which is good in one way, but disastrous in the other. The closer we get to the border, the more I break out in a cold sweat. From the inside pocket of my windbreaker, I take a box of tranquilizers that I had brought with me on purpose because I expected to be overcome with restlessness. I drink a few pieces, it will be enough to calm down a bit, without my reflexes going numb. However, you should be aware. You never know what to expect from someone. We finally arrived at customs.

- Do you have papers? - asks the Cop.

For fuck sake, they're going to crush us, I think to myself. Fatih is surprisingly calm, as if it's not the first time he's done this kind of thing, and maybe it's not, I'm getting more and more distrustful of him, even though there wasn't really any concrete reason for him to suddenly become suspicious. I guess because he was looking for more diamonds. He gives the Cop the papers, he sniffs something, rummages, tingles go through my body.

- Guys... Good luck, gentlemen. - says the Cop after some time, and I can't believe that we succeeded.

Inside I scream with joy and thank God a thousand times. The Cop didn't even look at my passport. Everything is going smoothly, at least once in this poor life of mine for the God to look at me. A little more and I'm free as a bird on a branch! Tatara ta ta ta

I tell the Cop through codes that everything went well and that we are at the agreed location.

LX

Soon there was a sound on my mobile phone, through which I communicated with the Cop. It was a photo of the other diamonds.

- Here, you can see how many there are. We will be rich - I say to Fatih.

He smiled, his eyes lit up when he saw the photo of the diamonds, but I was still tormented by some unbearable restlessness. Fatih's eyes seemed distant and I felt that something bad was brewing. In order to calm down, I suggested that we take a break for a cigarette and that I replace him while driving. He accepted.

- I'm buying a dealer soon, I told him after a certain period of dead silence.

He nodded his head to confirm that he had heard me. He entered the van into the merchandise section.

- You drive while I sort this out. - He said.

The part with goods in the van is physically separated, but you can pass through a small door into the inner part, so everything is connected in one segment. Time passed and I almost didn't reach the agreed place, where I buy the Cop. Fatih continues to rummage and arrange things in the back of the truck. It's a bit strange to me that he does so much, but I'm still afraid and I don't have time to think about it too much.

LXI

- There he is, Fatih. Are you done?
- Well, here it is. - he says, sweating all over.

I agree and the Cop enters the truck room.

- Petey – said Peter and offered Fatih his hand.
- Fatih. - replied the Bosnian.
- I'm glad.
- Me too. - they communicated laconically, as usually people from the world of drugs and crime do, because they don't know anything else besides that. Peter had already learned their language and knew how to pretend.
- To see the goods. - says Peter.

- Here, everything is there. - Fatih showed him the weapon boxes in which the drugs were stored:

- Shall I see the diamonds?

- Here. - I don't see what's going on, but I guess he showed him the diamonds.

I hear the sound of cardboard being pulled. He's obviously checking out the merchandise.

- And what is this? - I hear Fatih ask, and before he can answer, an exclamation: - Well, this is drugs! Where are the weapons, Dominik? - he shouts at me, and before I can come to my senses and say anything, I hear behind me: - There are weapons here.

I turn around and see that Fatih has put the gun to the Cop's temple and is holding him with his left hand around his neck.

- Now, take it easy, hand me the diamonds and turn your back. - he threatened him.

Darkness fell upon my eyes.

- Dominik, you fucking fraud! You will pay me for this! Sava and Danube will not wash you together. - shouted the Cop.

I didn't expect this. Fatih deceived me too. They will take the diamonds and the weed and kill the cop and me. Eh...

I knew something was going to happen when everything was going so smoothly for me.

LXII

It was raining like crazy; it's getting harder and harder for me to concentrate on driving, but I continue anyway. I can barely see; the windshield wipers can't even wipe the glass because the water falls literally in streams.
These two had calmed down for a while, but a commotion was heard again. I glanced over my shoulder to see what was happening and at that moment someone with a jeep came flying out of nowhere. I was nervous and almost crashed, but I kept driving. The shock caused the goods to fall in the back, and that was enough for the Cop to get out and snatch Fatih's gun. This one does not give in; they fight and fall over those boxes. I'm still driving, I'm not turning around. Fear overwhelmed me stronger than the rain that was falling. The best way to keep my head alive is to not get involved unless absolutely necessary. Whoever prevails, I will side with him, I have no other choice. Inside, I prayed to God that both of them would die. Suddenly a shot is heard.

-    You Arab motherfucker... - I hear the Cop cursing.
Fatih does not react.

-    Well, that's right. You sang the swan song. -
     continues the Cop, and it becomes clear to me
     that Fatih was killed.

What will happen to me now? Will they simply remove
me or put me behind bars? Now that he is going to let
me go - I don't believe that. The medicine is strong, and
I am terribly tired. Darkness falls on my eyes and I can
no longer see the road. One moment of inattention was
enough. The van hit the curb and we landed in the river.
The water kind of wakes me up, but the Cop got up too.
He grabbed me by the throat and pulled me into the back
of the truck. I don't know what force gave me strength
and I broke away from his grip. I quickly pushed him
forward and jumped on him. As we wrestle there, water
breaks in and the windows break. Dark.

LXIII

I don't know what happened in the last few minutes. Did
I faint, and the water pushed me to the surface by itself,
or did I have a hole in my memory from fear? Maybe I'm
dead and I don't know. I swim towards the edge of the

river and the fact that when I stop straining my body to make movements, I start to sink, is enough indication that I am still alive. I dragged myself to the shore with difficulty and lie down there, I couldn't even move anymore.

I have no idea how long I laid there. It could have been hours or a whole day. It was like I was under anaesthesia, and maybe I'm not in this world anymore, I thought. The rain was still falling, half of my body was drowned in mud and the other half was stained with it. The dampness and river grass gave off a foul smell. I turned my head to look at where I was, although I could hardly find the strength to stand up.

At that moment I saw the Cop lying on the beach, dead. If someone had told me that I would look forward to a certain death like my own wedding, I wouldn't have believed him. I gain some superhuman strength and stand up in a flash, light as a breeze, despite all the mud I'm dragging on my water-soaked suit and shoes. The Cop is lying on his back, without a belt, bare stomach. What a grotesque - and dead he bears the mark he had been running from all his life - he was nothing but a fat, muddy pig. I search his pockets and find a bag of diamonds. If only someone had seen my smile, then - I would have lit up the metropolis. It was a smile of freedom, a smile of final relief. The fat man also had a wallet with documents and a large sum of money in his pocket, close to a thousand euros and a few hundred Croatian Kuna. I take it and put it in my pockets, and then I bend down and pull the cop by the legs back into the river and let the current carry him away. The further and later they find him, the less suspicion I fall under.

It was already dark outside. God looked at me, so that I could more easily hide from the eyes of the world. I take the gun that was lying on the shore next to the dead cop and crawl out from under the bridge onto the road.

LXIV

I should have come up with something to civilize myself somewhere. The part where I came out was sparsely populated, and there were no shops even in the announcement. The first thing I had to do before that was to destroy all other evidence that could give away and lead to any connection with the Cop. I deleted all our conversations in my cell phone, took out the card, broke it and threw one half into the forest where I found myself, and the other some two hundred meters further down the bank. Then I threw the phone on some stone on the ground and crushed it with my foot, pouncing on it with all my strength from above and then spinning and pulling it with my foot to shred and trample every bit like my hateful past and then I buried it all deep under the ground and autumn fallen leaves .

I walked late into the night through the forest, until I saw a hunting cabin. I broke the door and went inside. I took off my muddy, wet clothes and put on some olive pants and a shirt, two sizes too big, that's all I found there. Then I opened the display case to see if there was anything to eat and the sun warmed me when I saw a tin of sardines. It seems to me - I ate it before I opened it. I then put the old clothes and the can into a bag I found there and lay down to rest for an hour or two until dawn.

I had some skill in locksmithing, since I used to fix everything at the old house in the absence of wages for craftsmen, so I also fixed the lock on the hunting cabin in an instant and closed everything as if no one had even come. From the traces of mud, they will notice that something is wrong, but no one will conduct an investigation because of a couple of rags and a can.

I walked about a mile until I reached the road. I wrapped that bag with old clothes and a can of sardines in a bush, and then started looking for the bus stop to go back to Zagreb. No more cops. I'm free. As for Fatih, I don't believe anyone will even ask. I actually did Adina a favour.

LXV

How many miles did I travel that night? I don't think I've ever hiked so much in my life and never been so tired. Whenever I was weak from fatigue, I would look into that bag and it gave me the strength to keep going, it reminded me that soon all the suffering will be over. When I finally saw the road and another bus coming and going in the direction of Zagreb, it seemed as if I was reborn. The bus stops and I get in:
- Excuse me, is this a bus to Zagreb? - I ask the driver as if I am interested, and I would go in any direction, just to get to a settlement.
- yes, it goes via Zagreb to Varaždin. - he answers and looks at me with messy, dirty hair in a suit that doesn't fit me at all, as if I fell from Mars, but I don't care.

- Thank you very much. – I cordially dissuade and pay the ticket with coins that I took from the Cop's pocket.

I sit in the last seat so as not to be the target of the curious eyes of grandmothers and alike. The bus starts, and I take the bag with diamonds from my chest and secretly open it slightly, just enough so that only my eyes can see the contents. I enjoy diamonds with all my senses.

Wow... This is for a new beginning - I speak to myself and the voice echoes and flows through my whole body. This is Dominik's sonata, this is the melody of freedom, I add in my mind.

Mom, I'm coming home!

I sing a toast to my old Ma and imagine her smile when she sees that I have returned to her alive and well.

Not far from the Croatian border with Bosnia, a van with Bosnian plates fell into the river. In it was found the lifeless body of a man of Bosnian nationality, about twenty-five years old, and among other goods - a package of about three hundred kilograms of marijuana. It is suspected that the young man is a member of a major dealer clan and that he is connected to a terrorist organization. Investigation underway

I hear the news on the radio, but I'm very tired. I put the bag of diamonds back under my shirt, fold my hands over the place where I placed them and slowly drift off to sleep.

To be continued . . .